"I can run for a long, long time yet."

Sara's voice was composed as she walked to the front door. But once the screen closed behind her, Mac heard her take the stairs two at a time.

It was good she'd left before he pulled her to him. Before he plundered her mouth with a thoroughness that would make her forget she was in a hurry to leave.

He cursed the cast that kept him pinned when he needed to pace until the image of Sara standing in moonlight faded along with his restlessness. Until the heady scent of roses that clung to her skin was replaced by the smell of sage and rangeland.

He must be very, very careful, he warned himself. Sara had proven she'd bolt when the going got really tough. He needed a team player. Definitely not a woman like Sara.

But how could he let her go?

Dear Reader,

To ring in 1998—Romance-style!—we've got some new voices and some exciting new love stories from the authors you love.

Valerie Parv is best known for her Harlequin Romance and Presents novels, but *The Billionaire's Baby Chase,* this month's compelling FABULOUS FATHERS title, marks her commanding return to Silhouette! This billionaire daddy is *pure* alpha male…and no one—not even the heroine!—will keep him from his long-lost daughter.…

Doreen Roberts's sparkling new title, *In Love with the Boss,* features the classic boss/secretary theme. Discover how a no-nonsense temp catches the eye—and heart—of her wealthy brooding boss. If you want to laugh out loud, don't miss Terry Essig's *What the Nursery Needs…* In this charming story, what the *heroine* needs is the right man to make a baby! Hmm…

A disillusioned rancher finds himself thinking, *Say You'll Stay and Marry Me,* when he falls for the beautiful wanderer who is stranded on his ranch in this emotional tale by Patti Standard. And, believe me, if you think *The Bride, the Trucker and the Great Escape* sounds fun, just wait till you read this engaging romantic adventure by Suzanne McMinn. And in *The Sheriff with the Wyoming-Size Heart* by Kathy Jacobson, emotions run high as a small-town lawman and a woman with secrets try to give romance a chance.…

And there's *much* more to come in 1998! I hope you enjoy our selections this month—and every month.

Happy New Year!

Joan Marlow Golan
Senior Editor
Silhouette Books

Please address questions and book requests to:
Silhouette Reader Service
U.S.: 3010 Walden Ave., P.O. Box 1325, Buffalo, NY 14269
Canadian: P.O. Box 609, Fort Erie, Ont. L2A 5X3

SAY YOU'LL STAY AND MARRY ME

Patti Standard

Silhouette

ROMANCE™

Published by Silhouette Books

America's Publisher of Contemporary Romance

TO STARR.
YOU KEPT THE PRESSURE ON.

 SILHOUETTE BOOKS

ISBN 0-373-19273-8

SAY YOU'LL STAY AND MARRY ME

Books by Patti Standard

Silhouette Romance

Pretty as a Picture #636
For Brian's Sake #829
Under One Roof #902
Family of the Year #1196
Say You'll Stay and Marry Me #1273

PATTI STANDARD

started her writing career after she stopped working full time and began an at-home typing service. She says that the brand-new word processor and all those blank disks were too tempting to ignore. Having been a romance fan since her teens, she decided that the time would never be better to try to put on paper the stories she'd been writing in her mind for years.

Patti also loves to travel. She says that she started with Hawaii when she was sixteen and has been going ever since. Her family knows that trouble is brewing when she spreads out her map collection on the living room floor. She lives in a small town in western Colorado at the edge of the Rocky Mountains with her children and husband.

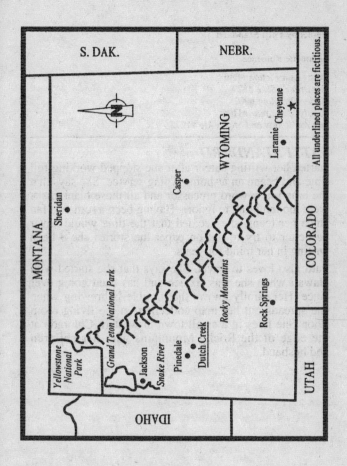

S. DAK.

NEBR.

MONTANA

WYOMING

Sheridan

Casper

Laramie   Cheyenne ★

Yellowstone National Park

Grand Teton National Park

Jackson

Snake River

Pinedale

Dutch Creek

Rocky Mountains

Rock Springs

IDAHO

UTAH

COLORADO

All underlined places are fictitious.

Chapter One

Sara Shepherd slammed the door and walked to the front of the truck, gravel crunching under her tennis shoes. She pushed sweaty bangs off her forehead with an exasperated shove as she watched steam hiss its way around the edge of the hood, the white wisps of vapor evaporating instantly in the dry Wyoming air. Gingerly, using the hem of her yellow T-shirt to protect her hand from the hot metal, she pulled the latch and lifted the hood. Steam billowed out, an antifreeze cloud escaping from a gash in a rubber hose connected to the radiator.

Sara cursed softly, using language her English professor husband would have dismissed as a sign of an inadequate vocabulary if he'd still been alive. That her dilemma was her fault only added to her frustration. She'd thought about buying extra belts and hoses before she left Denver last week, but had decided against it since the truck was only two years old. Leaving the hood propped open, she walked to the cab, stepped onto the running board and stuck her head in the window to look at the odometer.

Sixty-three thousand two hundred and fifty-eight miles—plus some odd tenths.

In two years.

Sara felt a combination of pride and dismay at the thought of all those miles, hard, compulsive, seldom-stopping miles from Canada to Mexico, east coast to west. And so many miles still ahead of her. She dropped to the ground and carefully tucked the edge of her T-shirt into her jeans. She surveyed the empty asphalt that snaked in both directions before disappearing in a shimmering haze of heat at the horizon. Not a car in sight.

Wyoming surrounded her, desolate, with only sparse grass and sagebrush corralled behind the miles of barbed wire fence that edged the narrow, two-lane highway. A stray gust of wind brought a windmill creaking to life behind her, forcing its rusted blades to make a desultory turn, movement enough to shake its weathered wooden frame all the way to the ground but not enough to raise so much as a drop of water to fill the empty stock tank at its base. Just looking at the alkali deposit that ringed the tank made her thirsty. She licked her lips as she tried to decide what to do.

A well-worn rut cut off the highway and crisscrossed its way to the distant mountains. It looked tempting, especially since Yellowstone National Park lay behind those mountains. She'd planned to reach Yellowstone sometime tomorrow after spending the night in Jackson Hole. But she knew that rut could just as easily peter out at some gully as lead to a house and telephone. Better to backtrack to that gas station she'd passed, Sara decided, hoping it was only a few miles back.

She took a long drink from the thermos in the cab, then grabbed her credit card and driver's license from her purse and stuffed the leather purse under the seat. She locked the truck's doors, double-checking that the door to the white camper covering its bed—her home for the past two years—was also securely locked. She started down the road, the asphalt under her feet soft from the afternoon sun, well aware that she left her entire life's possessions behind her.

The little gas station was closer than she remembered. It sat at the junction of two rural highways, alone except for a big white farmhouse ringed by shady cottonwood trees about a hundred yards behind the station. It was little more than a wide spot in the road, but the station's neat white siding and green shutters looked wonderful after a forty-minute walk. Two gas pumps squatted on a paved mat, sharing space with rainbow oil slicks and a pothole or two. The door to an attached garage yawned wide, and she could see a hydraulic lift inside, workbenches stacked with tools and thankfully, a collection of belts and hoses on hooks near the ceiling. She should be on her way to Yellowstone in a few hours, after all.

She pushed open the glass door to the station and set a bell jangling somewhere inside. A boy, perched on a stool behind the counter, looked up from his comic book at the sound. Maybe twelve or thirteen, he had an open, friendly face with freckles and a slight overbite that braces were trying to correct.

"Hi. I didn't hear your car."

"I'm on foot," Sara told him. "My truck's about two miles up the road with a blown water hose. I was hoping you could help me out."

"What year?" He dragged a dog-eared book from a shelf over the cash register and flipped it open on the scarred countertop.

She told him and described the location of the hose— by now she knew her truck intimately, inside and out. The boy thumbed through the pages, stopped at one, then followed a line of type across the page with his finger.

"Bingo! We've got one of those."

"Great." She relaxed and smiled with relief. She'd stubbornly tried to ignore her nervousness as she'd walked to the station. It hadn't helped that her daughter's warnings had come so easily to mind, keeping her company with each step. *I told you so,* the voice had said. *A grown woman driving around the country like some middle-aged hippy. It's just not safe, Mother.* And her mind had spun out the word *mother* in a perfect mimic of Laura, in that exasperated and exasperating tone her daughter had adopted since graduating from college.

Sara had only broken down once before, and it had been a simple flat tire. But she would think seriously about trading in her faithful blue truck for a new model when she passed through Denver this fall. A breakdown in the winter was something she didn't even want to contemplate.

"If you don't mind, I'll use your rest room for a minute while you ring that up. Add a bottle of that orange juice, too. It's going to be a hot walk back." She pointed to a cooler against the wall filled with drinks.

The boy's mouth fell open slightly, revealing even more of the braces. "You're going to walk to your truck?"

"I guess so." Sara smiled. "I didn't pass many taxis on my way here."

"But you're not going to fix it yourself," he protested.

"Sure I am. I'm pretty handy with a screwdriver. It shouldn't be hard."

He shook his head, adamant. "You can't walk all that way alone." He sounded truly concerned, and Sara was touched.

"It's not that far." She gave him another reassuring smile.

But he kept shaking his head, and fine brown hair sifted

into his eyes. "If my dad found out I let a woman walk off alone to fix a truck by herself, I'd be mucking stalls for a month. No, ma'am, you better wait here while I go get my dad. He'll drive you back."

"No, really, I'll—"

But he seemed determined. "You wait right here, ma'am. I'll go fetch my dad. He's up in the north field fixing some fence so it might be a minute or two. You just make yourself comfortable. Have that orange juice. I'll be right back."

He locked the register, grabbed a hat from a hook near the door and disappeared into the attached garage. Sara heard the roar of an engine and looked out the door. The boy had appeared in front of the station riding a three-wheeled motorcycle, a sturdy all-terrain vehicle with heavy, wide tires. He gestured to her and she pulled open the glass door and stepped outside.

"If anybody comes wanting to buy gas, you better have 'em wait for me to get back," he yelled over the engine. "There's not another gas station for forty miles, so they're not going anywhere." With a metallic grin and wave, he skidded around the side of the station and disappeared.

Sara rounded the corner after him and watched him head up a gravel lane toward the house. She had to smile at the sight of the boy, in jeans, cowboy hat and scuffed boots—every inch a cowboy—seated on the noisy machine as comfortably as on a horse. S-shaped irrigating tubes and a muddy shovel were strapped to the back of the ATV, bouncing at every rut.

Modern ranching. All helicopters and three-wheelers and million-dollar equipment. Not like when she was a kid growing up on a small farm on the outskirts of Denver, she thought with a twinge of nostalgia, when Denver still had traces of the real, honest-to-goodness cow town it used to be. Denver certainly had its share of cowboys even now, but that had more to do with fashion than with livelihood. She knew most of the Wranglers she saw had never touched a saddle.

Sara got a juice from the cooler and returned to the wooden bench that ran along the side of the station. She stretched out her legs to wait for her rescuer. It appeared chivalry wasn't dead, after all, she thought, taking a sip of the cold juice. Or at least not up here in the middle of Wyoming. Maybe there was still a sliver left of that famous cowboy code of the West. In spite of the ATV, the whole place seemed to be caught in some kind of 1950s time warp. She fanned aside a fly that buzzed lazily near her ear. The big old farmhouse, with its wide veranda just made for a porch swing and its huge swath of lawn, complete with shaggy lilac bushes, looked like something out of an old black-and-white western.

A memory drifted up, nudged to life by the Hollywood setting. Goodness, she hadn't thought of that endless summer in years. She'd been thirteen, horse crazy like all her friends, and for some reason she'd taken to reading Zane Grey books. She'd read every one, staying up long into the night when the house was as dark and silent as the heroes Grey wrote about. That teenage Sara had decided the long, lean, slow-talking cowboy was her kind of man. The hero was the same in every one of those classic westerns—concerned about his horse, concerned about his honor and devoted to his one true love. He never spoke more than a word or two to that true love throughout the book, but Sara had read volumes into the way he'd rolled his cigarette or the way he'd squinted into the horizon.

Sara squinted at the figure she saw appear from behind the ranchhouse, a horse and rider trotting down the lane toward her—her imaginary cowboy come to life. A man on a black horse, a man who sat in the saddle like he'd been born to it, a man with *spurs,* she saw as he reined to a stop in front of her and jumped to the ground with a jingle. Faded jeans, cracked leather belt, denim work shirt rolled back from his wrists, dark brown hair curling from underneath a dusty gray cowboy hat, face hidden by its brim—Zane couldn't have done better himself.

"Mac Wallace," he said, striding toward her. He slipped off a leather work glove and extended his hand.

"Sara Shepherd," she replied, noting the calluses as his big hand swallowed hers. Mac Wallace was several inches taller than she, and she had to tilt her head to meet his eyes, midnight blue eyes with intriguing lines fanning from the corners, testimony to years of outdoor work. Now that his hat no longer shadowed his deeply tanned face, she could see thick eyebrows, broad cheekbones, a square chin and the beginnings of an afternoon stubble. She breathed in the smell of horse and man sweat and was reminded once again of childhood summers.

"I hear you're having trouble with a water hose."

Sara nodded. "I told your son I could handle it, but he was kind enough to offer some help. I don't want to take you away from your work if you're—"

"No problem. We'll have you back on the road in no time."

The sound of the ATV returning caused the gelding to shy, and Mac quickly stepped back to grab the reins. "Damn machines. I hate them."

He soothed the horse with one hand while he made an impatient slicing motion with a finger across his throat. His son immediately cut the engine and coasted the rest of the way to the station to join them.

"Michael, take Justice to his stall and have your brother rub him down. I'm going to go fix Ms. Shepherd's truck." As the boy obediently swung into the saddle, Mac turned to Sara. "Do you have any water to refill the radiator?"

Sara nodded. "Five gallons."

"Antifreeze?"

She shook her head. "I better get a gallon or I'll overheat in the mountains for sure."

He escorted her inside the station, and she pulled her credit card from the back pocket of her jeans and laid it on the counter. Mac punched buttons on the cash register and handed her the receipt the machine spit out. She scribbled her signature.

"My truck's out front next to the mailbox," he said. "I'll get that hose and meet you there." He disappeared into the garage.

Sara looked at the receipt as she walked past the gas pumps to the gray truck parked beside the mailbox at the edge of the highway. She frowned.

"Mr. Wallace?" she began as he came toward her, minus the spurs but with a gallon of antifreeze in one hand and a black rubber hose in the other.

"Mac," he corrected, throwing them in the back of the truck and moving to open the door for her.

"Mac. This receipt doesn't show a charge for your repair service. Or the orange juice, either." He was very close. He stood beside her with a hand on the open door, his arm making a protective circle. Sara looked up from the receipt and was startled to find herself acutely, unexpectedly aware of the breadth of him, the warmth, the masculine, horsey smell. She felt a ridiculous urge to move closer into that circle. How long had it been since she'd stood, even casually, this near a man? Disturbed, she held out the white piece of paper.

But he didn't even glance at it. His eyes met hers. "There's no charge for being neighborly, ma'am."

"I thought making a profit from another's misfortune was the American way. And it's Sara."

"Well—Sara—that might be, but it's not my way."

She cocked her head and studied him, curious. Yet another example of cowboy chivalry, that fabled code? Finally, she said, "Then I thank you very much."

"My pleasure."

She found herself reluctant to look away from those dark, dark blue eyes. The moment lengthened, lasted for a heartbeat longer than it should have, that split second between a man and a woman when a look slides over the edge toward awareness. She was so aware of Mac Wallace she felt heat on her face and knew it came from more than the Wyoming sun. Embarrassed by her reaction, she folded the slip of paper, turning it again and again into neat squares, methodically creasing the edges, then tucked it into her pocket. Eyes lowered, she quickly stepped into the truck.

Mac shut the door and crossed behind the truck to the driver's side, smiling at the blush that had tinged the woman's cheeks, accenting her delicate features. He might spend his days surrounded by kids, cows and sweat-soaked leather, but he could still recognize healthy attraction in a woman's eyes when he saw it. Damn right. He pulled taut the blanket that covered the worn spot on the seat and slid behind the wheel.

"My truck's a couple of miles up that way." Sara pointed north.

"Headed for Yellowstone?" he asked as he turned onto the highway.

"Yes, I'm going to spend a few days there."

"Are you staying at the lodge? It's quite a place." He had spent his honeymoon there. A wonderful beginning to a dismal marriage.

Sara shook her head. "I've got a camper on my truck. But I do want to see the lodge. I've seen pictures of it and it looks charming."

Mac took his eyes from the road and looked at her more closely, wondering why a woman would choose to camp alone in Yellowstone. Especially a woman who used words like *charming*. He studied her profile as she watched the passing sagebrush from the window. She looked a couple years younger than his forty-five, and no makeup and the way her light brown hair was pulled into a ponytail made her appear younger still. Her features were fine, with an aquiline nose and high cheekbones that spoke of afternoon teas and painted china. *Charming*. Her patrician features were at odds with her jeans and tennis shoes, and he noted the way the tan on her left arm was more pronounced than on her right, typical of someone who spent a lot of time driving with an arm propped on an open window. Contradictions intrigued Mac.

"Are you from around here?" he asked.

"No, I'm from—" Sara hesitated, intriguing him even more. "I'm originally from Denver," she finished.

"You're not so far from home, then," he said.

"Not yet."

Her cryptic reply had him glancing at her again, and he found himself caught by the clouds he saw in eyes a misty shade of gray. "So you're going farther than just Yellowstone?"

She nodded. "I'll probably head into Canada, I think. I want to see Banff, even though it's supposed to be so commercialized now. Then maybe Calgary." She shrugged. "I'm not really sure yet."

"You're not sure where you're going?" He frowned. "You mean you're just...traveling?"

"Just traveling."

Mac could tell his questions made her nervous. She seemed relieved when her truck came into view.

"There it is."

He pulled behind the late-model, four-wheel-drive truck and camper. Sara jumped from his truck before he had time to open the door for her. Pulling a key ring from her pocket, she unlocked the door to the camper and unfolded a set of aluminum stairs. "I'll get that water," she said over her shoulder.

Mac peered into the camper through the open door. The compact space had a table and padded bench under one window and a tiny kitchen on the other side—although he wasn't sure he would call a sink the size of his cereal bowl, a shoe-box-size refrigerator and a two-burner stove exactly a kitchen. A mattress covered with a floral-print spread was tucked over the cab, and closets and storage bays cunningly crammed every spare inch. Like the inside of a doll house, everything was neat as a pin, almost clinically so, from the wrinkle-free bedspread to the paper towel roll with a perfectly torn edge centered on the wall above a miniature cutting board.

"Quite a setup you've got here," he said as Sara pulled a five-gallon water jug from a cupboard under the stove. He took the heavy container from her and helped her down the stairs.

"Everything I need."

"A little small, though."

"I prefer to think of it as cozy."

"Cozy like a turtle, maybe."

Sara laughed, and the sound was enough to stop him in his tracks. He looked at her, captivated again by her dove gray eyes, alight with humor.

"I guess it is," she said. "I've never quite thought of it that way. I just carry my home around with me wherever I go—like a turtle."

"I wouldn't call it exactly a home, would you? More like a hotel room. But it must be pretty convenient when you're on the road." He saw her smile fade and wondered. He started walking and set the water in front of the truck. "Let me get my toolbox and we'll start in."

Not a home? Sara patted the blue metal fender well protectively. It was the perfect home, as far as she was concerned. A thousand times more home than the neat brick house near the university where she'd lived for twenty years with her husband. Those bricks had formed walls so high they'd blocked her sun, cut off her air, made her fear they would tumble in on her at any moment, trapping her in the debris. But this, the metal under her hand warm and smooth, this truck and camper were freedom—and all the home she ever planned to have again.

She watched while Mac deftly removed the clamps, pried off the torn hose and slipped the new one in place. He filled the radiator with antifreeze and water and screwed the radiator cap tight.

"All set. Why don't you start 'er up, Sara, and let's make sure that new hose is going to do the trick."

Sara turned the key and the engine roared instantly to life. She smiled in satisfaction.

"Uh-oh." Her satisfaction was short-lived as she heard Mac's warning over the rumble of the engine.

"What's the matter?" She got out to stand beside Mac and stuck her head under the hood next to his. Her ponytail fell over her shoulder as she looked at the engine, the heavy-sweet smell of antifreeze making her wrinkle her nose. She followed his pointing finger and saw a small drop of water form along the bottom of a hose to the left of the radiator. The drop fattened, stretched, then fell to the ground. Another followed and another, making beads in the dust before collapsing to soak into the dirt.

"Maybe you spilled some water when you filled the radiator, and it's just running down that hose?" she asked hopefully.

But he shook his head. "It's another leak. You've probably had it a while and didn't even know it. You better drive to the station and I'll replace that hose, too. In fact, you ought to change out all your hoses if you're headed clear to Canada.''

Sara sighed and nodded. "You're right." She felt her teeth begin to worry the inside of her cheek and forced herself to stop the nervous habit. Another hour or so didn't make any difference. She'd still make Jackson in time to get a spot in a park, although it might be difficult this close to Yellowstone on a Friday evening in the middle of June. Well, she'd worry about it when she got there. If nothing else, two years on the road had given her a nonlinear perspective of time. Yesterdays and tomorrows tended to blend together. Straightening, she removed the metal rod and let the hood slam into place.

"I'll meet you at the station then," she said briskly.

"I'll be right behind you." Mac started for his truck and she allowed herself a moment to watch him while his back was to her, to appreciate the way he moved, confident and purposeful, with long strides that stretched his faded jeans in interesting ways around his hips.

Oh, for goodness' sake, she chided herself. Ogling the man like some sex-starved, premenopausal old woman. She shook her head at her thoughts and climbed behind the wheel, reminding herself that with a ranch and two sons—maybe more—there was sure to be a wife in a gingham apron somewhere inside that big white house.

Sara reached under the seat and pulled out her purse. She set it in its customary place, precisely in the middle of the bench seat between the seat belt fasteners. Then she adjusted the side mirrors and tilted the rearview mirror a minuscule degree. Her thumb brushed over the lighted radio panel to remove the slight film of dust that had accumulated during her drive north from Rock Springs.

There.

Perfect.

She slipped the truck into gear and guided it onto the highway, heading back the way she'd come.

A half hour later, Mac was tightening the last clamp. Sara watched from where she sat on the cool concrete floor, her back against the leg of a splintered workbench. He'd raised the truck on the hydraulic lift to reach an awkward hose and was standing under the engine, arms above his head. His work shirt was pulled tight across his back, the denim worn thin enough that she could see the outline of his muscles as they bunched and flexed in his shoulders. His biceps swelled with every twist of his wrist, and she stared, fascinated by the masculine rhythm.

The loud jingle of the station door opening made her blink, and she dragged her eyes away from their voyeuristic study. "It's, uh, it's pretty busy around here," she said. The bell had signaled a customer several times already, keeping Michael running between the pumps and the cash register.

"Weekends are good."

She saw Michael head out to check the oil on a red minivan. "Michael's certainly working hard. Do you have other children that help?"

"Jacob's up at the ranch right now." Mac muttered a quick curse as he tried to reach into a tight space.

"It must be tough to manage a ranch and a gas station at the same time," Sara said. Talk was better than silence, she'd decided, considering where silence seemed to lead her thoughts.

"It's not too bad. We only open the station in the summer—for the tourists. It's a way for the boys to earn college money." His voice echoed hollowly from inside the engine. "During the winter, we use the garage to repair the ranch equipment and store our fuel in the tanks. It beats running in to Dutch Creek every time you need gas."

"You're a long way from anywhere, all right." She shifted on the floor, pulling up her knees and wrapping her arms around them.

"Sometimes too far." He let out a puff of held breath as he gave a last twist to the screwdriver. "Sometimes not far enough." He ducked his head and peered at her. "Hey, Sara, bring me a soda from the cooler, will you? And get something for yourself if you want."

She got up and dusted off the seat of her jeans. "I still owe you for the last one."

"I told you, it's on the house."

"Not this time. And not for your work this time, either. I expect a hefty bill for all this."

Mac lowered his arms and grinned at her as he wiped his hands on a rag. "I'll get out my adding machine."

She went through the open door into the gas station, the whining of the lowering lift audible as she pulled open the foggy glass front to the soda case. "What kind does your dad like?" she asked Michael, who was at the cash register.

Before he could answer, Mac's shout ricocheted from the garage, followed by an ominous thud—then silence. Her eyes met the startled boy's. He sprang to his feet at the same time she turned, and together they raced into the garage.

"Mac?"

"Dad?"

Her truck was in the middle of the floor, innocently resting on its four wheels, but Mac was nowhere in sight.

"Mac?" Sara called again.

She rounded the truck, Michael at her heels, so close that he bumped into her when she stopped abruptly. Mac half-sat, half-lay on the cement, propped on his elbows, staring at his leg, his face pasty white. Sara's stomach did a flip as her gaze followed his and she saw the way his boot twisted outward at an unnatural angle.

He looked at her with a small, rueful smile. "It looks like this is going to be an expensive job for me, too."

Chapter Two

"Broken?" Sara asked, surprised at how calm she sounded since her heart thundered against her ribs, jolted by adrenaline.

"I'd say so." Mac was obviously trying to sound in control, as well, but the roughness in his voice belied the calm words.

"Michael, go get your mother, please." She laid a hand on the boy's shoulder and hoped it felt reassuring in spite of its tremble. "We better get your dad to a hospital."

Michael shook his head. He swallowed so hard his Adam's apple bobbed, but no sound came out. His mouth opened and closed futilely.

"His mother and I are divorced." A sheen of perspiration covered Mac's forehead. "Michael, I'm okay. Run up to the barn and tell Jacob to get down here—see if we can pry me off this floor. Go on, now. I'm okay."

Movement returned to the boy's stunned limbs and he was out of the garage in a flash, running as if his father's life depended on it.

Sara looked helplessly at Mac. "What happened?" She moved to kneel beside him, afraid to touch him but instinctively wanting to be close.

"Tire caught my boot when she came off the lift."

Sara looked at his twisted foot, horrified. "You mean my truck landed on your foot?"

"Just the tip of my boot, but it knocked me off balance." He joined her in staring at his foot, now free of the tire. "Leg went one way, foot went the other."

She felt sick at the thought and her stomach lurched again. "I'm *so* sorry. This is all my fault."

"It's not your fault."

"Of *course* it is!" She reached toward him, then pulled back, her hand wavering in the air. "You were doing the code of the west thing, with the hat and spurs and all, just like Zane Grey, and look what happened! This is all my fault. Here, let me help you—"

Mac was trying to push himself up by sliding his hands forward a fraction at a time.

She could tell the movement was excruciating. She tried to support his back without jarring his leg. "Better?"

He nodded, a jerky little bob as if he was afraid of any larger movement. "Thanks. Now, what's all this about Zane Grey?"

Before she could answer, she heard the thud of running feet, then two boys dashed into the garage, breathless.

"Jeez." Jacob appeared older than his brother but had the same straight brown hair and country-scrubbed look, like he'd been hung to dry in the sun. His looks were at odds with the strong barnyard odor that clung to him, and Sara guessed he'd been mucking those same stalls Michael had worried would be assigned to him.

"Is it broken?" He echoed Sara's words.

"Yeah. Call the Swansons and ask Libby to drive me into Dutch Creek."

Jacob shook his head. "They're in Cheyenne, remember? The Cattlemen's Association meeting."

"Well, call the Reeds then. See if Robby can—"

"They're in Cheyenne, too. At the—"

"Right, the Cattlemen's Association meeting." Mac's shoulders were rigid with tension.

"I can drive you, Dad," the boy offered.

"No way."

"Come on," Jacob pleaded. "I'm fourteen. This is an emergency, for cripe's sake. I'll go real slow. I can do it, Dad."

"Jacob, you don't have a license. You can drive around the ranch all you want but you're not going on the highway, and I don't feel like having this discussion right now. Try Joe over at—"

"Is my truck fixed?" Sara interrupted.

All three turned to her in surprise, as if they'd forgotten she still knelt beside Mac, her hand touching his back.

Mac said, "It's all set."

"Then, gentlemen, let's help your father up and see if we can maneuver him into the cab." It was the least she could do, she thought. This was all her fault. She should have replaced those hoses in Denver. The truck should have been perfect before she left Laura's. Perfect.

She stood and eyed the boys, both several inches taller than her own five-foot-five and quite a few pounds heavier. "One on each side," she directed, "and let him put all his weight on your shoulders until he gets his good leg under him."

Mac immediately protested, "Sara, we can manage. I'll just call one of the neighbors and—"

"It sounds like they're all in Cheyenne to me, and besides, I'm headed for Dutch Creek, anyway." She smiled. "I'll just push you out the door in the hospital parking lot. You won't even slow me down."

Mac's answering grin was weak. "Since you put it that way, thank you."

"Thank me once we get you up. I don't think this is going to be pleasant. Ready, boys?"

Hesitant but determined, they positioned themselves beside their father. Mac put an arm around each shoulder and slowly, carefully, they stood, lifting him to his feet.

Sara could almost hear his teeth grind as he tried not to yell when his broken ankle shifted and the weight of his boot pulled on it. He blanched again and his jaw twitched spasmodically.

"Are you okay?"

Mac grunted and took a deep breath. He let it out slowly, hissing between clenched teeth, "Let's go."

With a half-hop, half-shuffle, the boys helped him around the pickup to where she held open the passenger door. Mac put his good foot on the running board and managed to heave himself sideways onto the seat, leaving both legs stuck out the door.

Michael appeared near tears as he watched his father inch backward, dragging his injured foot inside the cab bit by bit.

"Michael," Sara said to the younger boy, hoping to distract him, "see if you can find something soft for your father to rest that foot on. It might swell less if it's propped up."

"There's cushions on those chairs next to the counter," he suggested, already turning.

"That should do the trick. Speaking of swelling, I wonder if we should try to get that boot off."

"Don't touch it!" It was clear Mac's shout was involuntary.

She glanced at the heavy leather boot, obviously of high quality in spite of signs of wear. "I'd hate for them to have to cut off your boot, that's all."

"Nobody's cutting off my boot!" He sounded even more alarmed. "Michael, you just put those pillows on the floorboard there and I'll be fine." He'd backed up until he was almost opposite the steering wheel, his legs still pointed toward the door. Michael piled three canvas-covered pillows on the floor, and slowly Mac slid his injured left leg off the seat to rest on the stack, as straight as the cramped confines of the cab allowed. He bent his right leg at the knee and pulled it in far enough for Sara to shut the door.

"Michael, take care of the station," he called through the open window, "and Jacob, be sure to finish Justice's stall. And take a shower."

"Can't we come with you?" Michael asked, still worried but trying hard not to show it. "Maybe we could ride in the camper?"

"There's no sense you hanging around the hospital. You'd have to stay in the waiting room the whole time. I'll phone you as soon as I get there and have somebody in town run me home."

"But—"

Mac ignored his interruption. "I'll only be gone a couple hours. They'll stick me in a cast, hand me some crutches, and I'll be home in time to fix supper. Scratch that, I'll pick up a couple of pizzas, okay?"

"You'll call?" Michael stood on the running board and leaned through the window.

"I'll call." Mac reached out to ruffle his hair. "And you call the hospital and tell them we're coming in so they can track down the doctor. Sara, you ready?"

She tried to slide behind the wheel, only to find her hip and shoulder come up firmly against Mac. She had to press herself against the length of him in order to squeeze in enough to shut her door.

"Do you have enough room?" He started to shift over

but a sharp intake of breath told her how much the effort cost him.

"You hold still. Just let me fasten my seat belt." She groped awkwardly behind him until she managed to press the metal clip of her seat belt into the fastener that poked into Mac's hip. Her fingers were clumsy with embarrassment as they fumbled against the back of his jeans, and she knew her cheeks reddened.

After turning the key to start the engine, she reached out to adjust the rearview mirror, but stopped herself halfway. No time for that. No time for the little ceremonies that so easily became habit. No time to make everything perfect. Ignoring the unease she felt at skipping the ritual, she shoved the truck into gear, her hand brushing along Mac's thigh with every movement, and backed out of the garage.

Mac waved to the boys, who stood forlornly in the open door of the garage, and Sara guided the truck onto the highway, avoiding as many jarring potholes as she could.

As soon as they rounded a curve in the road, putting the garage out of sight, she felt Mac slump heavily against her. His shoulders rounded inward as he hunched against the pain.

"Damn," she breathed, suddenly realizing his cheery wave had been an act for the boys' sake. "How far to Dutch Creek?"

"Forty miles."

"I'll drive fast."

"Good."

They were silent, the only sound the growl of the truck's engine as she accelerated well past the speed limit. The door handle dug uncomfortably into her hip and she shifted in her seat. The imperceptible movement brought her into even closer contact with Mac.

"Sorry," she said.

"That's okay." He made an obvious effort to collect himself. "Look, we're going to be pretty close for the next forty-five minutes, so we might as well be comfortable." He put his arm across the back of the seat behind her head, giving them extra inches of shoulder room. "Now, you lean into me and I'll lean into you, and we'll sort of prop each other up."

Sara tried to relax against him but so many nerve endings tingled from his nearness she felt her muscles stiffen and contract rather than relax. The feel of his forearm so close behind the bare skin of her neck, the sight of his fingers curved loosely near her shoulder, the way she nestled so perfectly under his arm—

"So, now that I'm a captive audience—"

Mac's voice made her jump, she'd been so engrossed in the unique sensations flooding her body, her unexpected reactions to the man.

"—we might as well get to know each other a little better. Tell me something about Sara Shepherd."

She stared at the mountains ahead of her, a little closer, a sharper outline against the brilliant blue sky. The wind whipped in the window, teasing strands from the elastic band securing her ponytail. "I'm forty-three," she began, pulling a wisp of hair from her mouth and pushing it behind her ear. "Grew up on a farm outside of Denver. Married young. Widowed for four years now. One child, a daughter named Laura. She's twenty-four."

She stopped. Over twenty years summed up in little more than a breath. Mac seemed to be waiting for more, but she suddenly could think of nothing else to say. Married, widowed, one child. The life of Sara Shepherd.

"That's all? A succinct curriculum vitae if I ever heard one."

She smiled. "Trying to impress me with your Latin, huh? Reminds me of a professor friend of my husband. He likes to sprinkle his speech with a little quid pro quo now and then.''

"It's a habit I picked up from an old English professor of mine at the University of Wyoming.''

She looked at Mac in surprise. "The University of Wyoming? You can't mean Cyrus Bennington?''

"Don't tell me you know Cyrus?''

"Know him? I just spent two days visiting him in Cheyenne! He and my husband were very close. My husband was an English professor at the University of Denver.''

"How about that!'' Mac exclaimed. "Cyrus and I have been friends since my college days. He comes out here every August, trades in that English driving cap of his for a Stetson, lights up a stogie instead of his pipe and plays cowboy for a week or so.''

She laughed. "Now that I can't picture. Cyrus with a secret life. He's never mentioned it.''

"Small world, huh?'' Mac's smile made the lines around his eyes crinkle even more, and Sara found herself wanting to take her eyes from the road often to look at him.

"So now that we've discovered we're almost related,'' he said, "I think you can enlarge a little on that life's story of yours, don't you?''

She shook her head. "It will bore you to tears—put you right to sleep.''

"A woman with a face like a cameo angel driving a truck all alone to Canada? I don't think so.'' She could feel his gaze slide over her features and her heart skipped a nervous beat. "To tell you the truth,'' he went on, "if you put me to sleep I'd be grateful. And don't bother to wake me up when we get to the hospital, either. Whatever they're going to do to me, I think I'd rather be asleep.''

Guilt stabbed through her again. If listening to her talk would take his mind off his ankle, give him something to concentrate on besides the pain, she'd gladly talk from here to Dutch Creek.

"You want my whole life's story then?"

"Start with the 'just traveling' part." Mac laid his head against the seat and closed his eyes. "How long have you been just traveling?"

"Two years."

"Two years!" His eyes flew open and he turned his head sharply to look at her, jarring his leg. "Ow!" He set his boot more securely on the stack of pillows. "I was thinking more along the lines of a couple of weeks."

"Nope. Two years."

"You've been traveling around the country, living in your camper, for two years?"

She nodded.

Mac settled against the seat once more like a child awaiting a favorite story. "Okay, start from the beginning."

The beginning? She wasn't sure there was a beginning. When had her life with Greg began to seem like a trap rather than a marriage? When had the dishes and the laundry and the PTA bake sales combined to drag her down until she had no idea how to lift herself up any more?

"I guess things sort of came to a head when Laura graduated from college." She took a firmer grip on the steering wheel as she tried to pick her way through the debris of the past. "My husband had been dead for two years by then, and I was still living in Denver. Most of our friends had really been Greg's friends, it turned out, and I found myself alone a lot. All alone in that house." Her voice tightened. "That house. Dusting that same damn china every week, vacuuming that mile-long carpet in the living room—vanilla cream carpet—washing those blinds with all those metal slats, row after row of them, catching every particle of dust—" She broke off as she saw Mac looking at her curiously. She consciously relaxed her jaw, which had tensed at the memories.

"Anyway, when Laura graduated from college, I said enough. I threw in the suburban-housewife towel. Sold the house, the lawn mower, the matching china— I had a yard sale you wouldn't believe. Sold every last thing." She found herself smiling. Just the thought of ridding herself of the shackles of her previous life could still make her breathe easier, more freely. Twenty-two years worth of clutter—all gone.

Mac saw the smile and couldn't comprehend it. He still had his merit badges from Boy Scouts, Jacob's first baby tooth, his father's World War Two duffel bag. Those possessions grounded him, defined him, located him and his space in the impersonal scheme of things. They were the physical, tangible record of a life, and no one sold a life at a yard sale.

He said, "I don't believe it. Not everything. You couldn't have sold your daughter's baby book."

"Of course not!"

Aha! He'd known it.

"I gave it away."

"What?"

"I gave all that kind of personal stuff to Laura. Passed it on to the next generation, so to speak. Those things are important to Laura. All I've got left is three pairs of shoes, a few pairs of jeans, enough dishes to fill a strainer, a CD player..." She paused and appeared to think for a moment. "That's about it. Oh, and a spider plant."

"A decadent luxury."

Sara laughed. "I'm managing to keep it alive."

The throbbing in his ankle reached clear to his hip by now, but he ignored it, concentrating instead on this woman beside him who'd pared her life down to an unrecognizable skeleton. "You mean there's no dog to share the campfire with? No collection of matchbooks from places like Sweettooth, Texas? No knitting bag with a half-finished chartreuse pillow cover?"

She shook her head. "I read a lot."

"Hmm." He scratched the back of his neck absently. They came up on an eighteen-wheeler and Sara passed the huge truck without loosing speed. Smooth. Controlled. Crossing and recrossing the white line with practiced skill—two years of practice. The more she told him, the more he wanted to probe.

"So you sold everything, got into your truck and headed—where?"

"It didn't matter at the time. I guess it still doesn't. Into the sunset sounded good as far as I was concerned. I drove to the closest interstate entrance, and since I didn't want to make a left into traffic, I took a right. And right was north." She rested her elbow on the open window and drummed her fingers against the outside of the door, occasionally letting the force of the wind lift her hand and push her palm open. It was as if she caressed the air, savored the motion, as she described that first dash to freedom.

"It was the middle of July, blastingly hot, so I kept on going north. Seattle, British Columbia, then skirted the northern states, Minnesota, New York, Maine. I ran out of land in Bar Harbor and it was starting to get cold so I turned south. By November I was somewhere in Georgia. I spent that winter in the south avoiding the snow, then when it warmed up I headed north again. Sort of a big, looping circle."

"Sounds like the way herds migrate."

She smiled. "I guess."

He tried to understand. "But herds follow the food, the grass. What did you follow? What *do* you follow?" He studied her as she kept her eyes on the road, the asphalt singing beneath the tires. What siren's song did she hear?

"It still doesn't matter. There's no destination to this trip." She sounded very sure. He knew she'd already asked herself the same questions. "As long as I never have to write another to-do list as long as I live, I'll be happy. No schedule, no have-tos, no responsibilities, no one depending on me—"

"But what about your daughter?" Where was the room for family in a one-woman camper? he wondered.

"Laura." Sara sighed. "She's a grown woman. She's got a college degree, a good job, her own apartment, her own life—but she considers the way I live some kind of personal affront."

"She doesn't approve?"

"That's putting it mildly. She thinks I'm nuts, having some kind of mid-life crisis or something, and I'll snap out of it if she badgers me long enough. Go back to baking cookies or whatever it is she thinks I should be doing."

"Oh." Mac tried to sound noncommittal. Obviously he failed.

"And what does that mean?" Her eyes were narrowed against the lowering sun, hair tangling in the wind, golden strands mixed with the brown. "You think I'm nuts, too?"

"I didn't say that," he hedged. "But you have to admit it's not your run-of-the-mill life-style."

"Haven't you ever had days when you wanted to say to hell with it all—" she waved a hand to encompass the road, the land, all of Wyoming "—and just take off for the tropics?"

Had he ever wanted to bolt? Mac considered her question. There had been a time, those nights right after his wife had left, when he'd sit at the too-silent supper table looking at his boys over the charred pot roast, dishes from last night still piled in the sink, the boys ready to burst into tears or fights at the drop of a pin. Could he have walked out?

He shrugged. "I've lived in the same house all my life. My father and grandfather were born upstairs. My great-grandfather homesteaded the land I work today." He shook his head. "I can't imagine living anywhere else. I can't imagine wanting to be anywhere else."

Sara was silent a moment. "You're lucky," she said finally.

"I'm very lucky." He knew he was. He might be tied to the land, but the ties were velvety soft and he willingly slipped his hands into the straps every time he plunged a shovel into the dark soil, every time he singed the Wallace brand into the hide of a bawling calf, every time he broke ice on a watering trough. Every time he dragged on his boots, tugged on his gloves, slapped his hat on his head and slammed the screen door, a door that had been slammed by four generation of Wallaces, he pulled the straps tighter, and more comfortably, around him.

"I'm not saying that ranching's for everyone, either," he felt compelled to add. "My ex-wife certainly didn't think so. It's hard work, the money's lousy, and the winters are hellish."

"But you love it."

"I do."

"She didn't?"

"No, she didn't." He knew Sara waited for more, but he refused to elaborate. He didn't like to talk about Ronda. He didn't like to think about Ronda.

"Oh, so I'm supposed to tell all but you get to be the strong, silent type? Nothin' doin'."

"Ask me about something else then." He saw the spec-ulative look Sara gave him but was relieved when she dropped the subject of his ex-wife. His foot pounded in time to his pulse and he had to concentrate to keep his muscles relaxed. His marriage wasn't something he could talk about without stiffening up until he was one big cramp.

"All right," she agreed, "what does Mac stand for?"

"MacKenzie."

"MacKenzie Wallace. A good clan name."

"Quite a few generations back, but my father was proud of it. Being an only child, he made sure I'd carry on the name. Whereas you—" he looked at her carefully "—I'd say you're from solid English stock."

"And how can you tell that?"

His arm still lay along the back of her seat, and he reached up to trail a finger lightly along her cheekbone. "It's that peaches and cream complexion of yours, like a rose petal settled right here—" He traced his way slowly up to her ear, suddenly unable to stop what had started as a casual touch. His blood quickened and he forgot all about the pain in his ankle. He wanted to let his finger slip down the curve of her neck, follow her collarbone, dip inside her T-shirt—

He jerked his hand away and curled his fingers around the back of the seat, gripping the padded upholstery tightly. The pain in his ankle roared to life, exploding from a dull ache to a white-hot throb, but the groan that welled from a place down deep inside came more from the unexpected and unwelcome feeling of desire than from physical pain.

He cleared his throat and tried to sound as if the touch of her silken skin under his fingers had left him unaffected. "You know, the English were bitter enemies of the Scottish clans. I bet my ancestors and yours were pretty nasty to each other."

Sara's cheeks were tinged a delicate pink, but her voice was calm as she said, "So I've heard. They wouldn't approve of my aiding and abetting the enemy this way. Although I guess since it was my truck that injured you in the first place, I struck my blow for England.''

"It was quite a blow." He pointed to the cluster of buildings that had come into view as the truck reached the top of a small rise. "Take a left at the stop sign. The hospital is right behind the high school."

They were at the small clinic within minutes, a single-story cinder-block building painted sterile white. Sara parked directly in front of the double glass doors, ignoring the yellow-striped parking spaces on the other side of a low brick planter.

"Wait here. I'll get somebody to help you."

Sara jumped from the truck and disappeared inside. She was back almost immediately, followed by a nurse pushing a wheelchair.

"Afternoon, Susie. How are you?" he greeted her. Susie wore her usual no-nonsense white uniform covered by a shapeless, colorless sweater. She was as wide as she was tall, and her faded brown hair curled tight to her scalp like sheep's wool. She'd been playing around with those home perms again, he saw.

"Mac Wallace, what have you done to yourself?" She yanked open the truck door and stood with her hands on her massive hips, her look disapproving.

"Have you been losing weight again?" he asked. "I swear, you're going to disappear on me one of these days."

"That didn't work when you were a kid trying to get out of a shot, and it won't work now. Come on, let's haul your butt out of there." She took off her wire-rimmed glasses and let them dangle from the gold chain around her neck, motioning with her hands. "Scoot forward. Try to take your weight on your good leg."

He couldn't believe the agony caused by the slightest movement. His denim shirt was soaked with sweat by the time he'd maneuvered himself into the wheelchair. He took a deep breath, steadying himself, before he looked at Sara. She stood in front of him, beside her blue truck, uncertain, looking as worried and as near tears as Michael had. He tried to smile reassuringly.

"Thank you," he said.

She nodded. "You're welcome." The silence lengthened while Mac stared into dove gray eyes, suddenly hesitant to say goodbye.

"The doctor's waiting for you," Susie said, releasing the brake on the chair. "And he's not too pleased about having his fishing interrupted, so we better get a move on." She started to turn the chair to the door.

"Goodbye," Sara called. She lifted a hand in a half-wave.

"Goodbye. Thanks again." The chair faced the hospital entrance, and he could see Sara's reflection in the glass doors. He watched her walk around the truck before the automatic opener on the hospital doors swung them wide, stretching her image until it broke and disappeared. He heard the truck door slam and the engine start as Susie pushed him over the threshold into the cool, antiseptic hallway. His teeth began to chatter. Delayed shock, he told himself, clamping his mouth shut. The empty feeling in his gut had nothing to do with loneliness.

Sara pulled into the hospital parking lot an hour later. Instead of heading down the highway, she'd had a hamburger from a drive-through ice cream stand and wandered around the four-block main street of Dutch Creek, self-proclaimed gateway to Yellowstone National Park. Miniature stuffed buffaloes and gaudily dyed geodes seemed to be the tourist merchandise of choice, along with the ever present T-shirts.

She'd followed the sidewalk past the last shop—a combination frozen-yogurt-southwestern-pottery store—to the park at the end of the street. She'd sat on a bench next to the empty playground under the shade of a cottonwood tree and worried about Mac. After a half hour of internal debate, she'd walked to her truck and returned to the hospital, unable to drive away without checking on him.

She felt guilty, she decided. That was why she was so reluctant to leave. It had nothing to do with the way his hand had lingered on her face that brief moment in the truck, his roughened fingertips gentle against her skin. She just needed to be sure he'd been released and was on his way to the ranch. Just a quick stop at the front desk was all it would take. She'd make it to Jackson Hole before dark.

But the admissions desk was shuttered when she entered the hospital, and there was no bell on the counter under the hand-lettered please-ring-for-service sign. A single hallway stretched before her, its waxed gray vinyl reflecting the overhead fluorescent lights, the walls a no-nonsense, industrial-strength green. She started down it, searching for the nurse's station.

Mac's voice was audible after only a few feet, coming from an open door at the end of the hall. She peeked around the edge of the frame. A narrow hospital bed, both foot and head raised, took up almost all of the tiny room, and Mac took up almost all of the bed. His one-size-fits-all beige gown came only as far as his knees, so the old-fashioned, white plaster cast, molded from mid-calf to toes, was the first thing to draw her eyes. The intravenous drip attached to the back of his hand was the next.

Mac was shouting into the perforated circle in a metal panel on the wall near his head. He held a cord in his free hand and was viciously poking the white button at its end with his thumb.

"Susie, this is the last time I'm saying this, I want to go home!"

Sara heard the nurse's voice echo from the panel, impatience clear despite the scratchy intercom.

"You can't go home, Mac. Now settle down before I come give you another shot of something. And stop pushing that buzzer."

"The boys are home by themselves. I can't just lay here. I've got to get home."

"Listen, I'll call the Swansons and have Libby go over—"

"They're in Cheyenne."

"At the Cattlemen's Association—"

"Yeah, yeah," he interrupted. "Now bring me my clothes and the only boot that damned doctor didn't mutilate and—"

"Mac, the doctor said we need to keep an eye on you overnight. I can't do a thing about—"

"I can stay with them."

Mac's head shot around at the sound of her voice.

"What was that, Mac?" Susie asked over the intercom.

"Just a minute, Susie. I'll buzz you."

"You touch that buzzer one more time and I'll—"

Mac flicked the switch on the wall, cutting off the nurse's threat.

"Hi." He looked at Sara as if nothing would surprise him anymore. "I thought you'd gone."

"I came back." She didn't elaborate.

"Oh." He paused. "Did you know that damned doctor cut off my boot? Elephant. Genuine elephant. It's not like you can go down to the local five-and-dime and get another elephant hide boot!"

"I'm sorry. They looked like nice boots."

"Damn right! And now they've got me pumped so full

of painkillers they say they want to keep me overnight so they can drip it into me drop by drop!''

''Mac, I'd be happy to go to the ranch and stay with the boys,'' she said. Why not? That was the whole point of her new life—no schedule, no worries, no one to answer to. If she could help out someone who'd helped her, what did it matter if she took a day longer to get to Yellowstone? ''Besides, I still owe you for that last batch of repairs. I could keep an eye on the boys tonight, come pick you up in the morning, and we can settle the bill then.''

''I can't have you go to all that trouble.'' Mac bounced his good leg against the mattress in frustration. ''There's got to be *somebody* who didn't go to Cheyenne for the weekend.''

''You'd be doing me a favor, really,'' she told him. ''It'll be difficult finding an RV spot this late in Jackson. I need a place to park.''

''It's nice of you to offer, Sara, but...'' Mac hesitated and she was surprised to see a look of embarrassment on his face. Of course! She realized the problem with a start. That time they'd shared in the truck had made her feel so close to him, she'd forgotten they were strangers. She couldn't ask him to leave his children in the care of someone who'd wandered into his gas station mere hours before.

''But I could be a mass murderer or something?''

''I don't mean that, but—''

''Hey, you can't be too careful these days. You're absolutely right. I'd feel the same way in your place.'' Sara thought for a moment. ''I tell you what, why don't I give Cyrus a call over at the university? He'll vouch for my sanity.''

''Any friend of Cyrus's is a friend of mine?'' Mac thought it over for a moment. ''Sure, sounds like a good idea. Of course, it could be the morphine talking, but right now all I want is to go to sleep and I can't think of any other alternatives."

Mac did look tired, sick-tired, with dark smudges under his eyes. Sara picked up the phone next to his bed and dialed the number of her late husband's oldest and dearest friend.

"Cyrus?" She was pleased to hear his voice after only the first ring. "You'll never guess who I ran into in Dutch Creek."

"Mac Wallace," he replied promptly in his crisp English accent. When she gasped, he said, "My dear girl, there are only a dozen people living in that entire half of the state. It wasn't exactly a stumper."

She laughed. Cyrus always made her feel good. Briefly, she explained the situation, then handed the phone to Mac. "He wants to talk to you."

Sara could hear only one side of the conversation, but Mac laughed out loud several times. She could just imagine what Cyrus was telling him about her.

"All right, Cyrus," Mac said. "I'll keep that in mind. It's been great talking to you. The boys can't wait to see you in August." He held out the phone for her to hang up.

"Well?"

"Cyrus said you're definitely sane, the salt of the earth, he'd trust you with his children any time—if he had any—and he urged me to marry you immediately."

Chapter Three

"He what!"

"His exact words were, 'Please pry that lovely child from that vile truck and wed her *immediatus,* which I think loosely translates into pronto."

"Or, if your Latin's as good as mine, could mean 'when hell freezes over.'"

Mac grinned. "Cyrus has been trying to get me remarried for years. He thinks it's my dumb luck that you happened into my garage and said I shouldn't look a gift horse in the mouth."

"I'm a gift horse?" She tried to sound lightly amused in spite of the way her heart had jolted at Cyrus's eccentric suggestion.

"I was sort of paraphrasing what he actually said. He lost me when he started quoting Julius Caesar." Mac's smile faded. "Seriously, Cyrus said I should jump at your baby-sitting offer. So I'm jumping—as high as I can under the circumstances. And I really want to thank you for your help."

"That's all right. As a man once told me when he fixed my water hose for free, it's just being neighborly."

His look was warm and she felt unreasonably pleased by his gratitude. She felt as if she'd done something wonderful, rather than simply offered to baby-sit in exchange for a parking place. His blue eyes held hers, and she read things in them she told herself came from the morphine, not from Mac. Things that made the narrow hospital bed suddenly appear plenty wide enough for two, if she was pressed up tight enough against him... Discomfited, she picked up the phone and held it out to him. "Here, call the boys and tell them I'm coming—with pizza."

"They like pepperoni."

"Got it." It was as hard to leave him now as it had been in the parking lot. "Is there anything I can do for you before I go? I think your nurse sounded pretty serious about not touching that buzzer again."

"Not unless you happen to have an extra elephant-hide boot tucked away in that camper of yours."

"Sorry, it's just me and my spider plant, remember?"

"Then I guess I'll see you tomorrow." His inflection made it a question, a lonely-sounding question. The small hospital seemed quiet and empty, no ringing phones, no gurneys whisking down the corridors on rubber wheels, no clipboards crisply snapping shut.

"I'll ask what time they think you'll be released. Try to get some sleep now." Impulsively, she took his hand and gave it a reassuring squeeze as she dropped a light kiss on his cheek. But his skin was so firm and warm, with his shadow of whiskers prickling her sensitive lips, that an erotic jolt caught her unaware. She jerked upright and stepped away from the bed. Murmuring good-night, she walked quickly from the room before she found an excuse to linger any longer, her mouth still hot and tingling.

She arrived at the ranch just over an hour later. The sun

hovered on the horizon, fiery layers of pink, orange and mauve, as she guided the truck up the gravel drive and pulled around the side of the two-story house. She walked up the wooden steps that led to the porch, balancing two large, flat pizza boxes.

Michael answered her awkward knock on the back door, delivered with the toe of her tennis shoe.

"Hi. Come on in." He took the boxes from her and politely moved aside for her to enter.

His older brother stood in the kitchen, hair still wet from a shower. Jacob looked at her a little warily. She was sure the boys wished she were Libby—the name that had come first to everyone's mind when Mac had needed help—rather than some stranger who'd been dropped in their laps. At their age, they didn't need an adult hovering over them, making sure they brushed their teeth before bed, so she hastened to reassure them that she wouldn't intrude.

"I just wanted to deliver these pizzas." She stayed at the threshold. "Your dad said you liked pepperoni."

They nodded and smiled stiffly.

"I'm all set up for the night in my camper—" she started to back away "—but if you men need anything, be sure to give a knock on the door."

"Aren't you going to have some pizza?" Michael asked, obviously surprised.

She shook her head. "I had a hamburger in Dutch Creek. Good night, then."

"But Dad said to put clean sheets on the bed in the guest room," Michael blurted. "And we even changed the towels in the bathroom."

She tried not to smile. "That was sweet of you, but—"

"At least come in and have a cup of coffee," Jacob offered. "Dad said to have some ready for you. I made a whole pot, and me and Mike don't like it."

"*I* like it," Michael said.

"You like the cream and sugar," his brother scoffed. "It's a wonder your teeth haven't rotted off under those braces."

"Thank you." Sara stepped into the kitchen before the argument escalated. "A cup of coffee would be nice."

Jacob sat the pizza boxes in the middle of the large butcher-block table while Michael rather defiantly got out two mugs. She poured them both a cup of coffee without comment, although she spooned a generous amount of sugar and creamer into her cup so Michael's lavish use of both wasn't so obvious.

"Does he have a cast or just one of those bandage things?" Michael asked, dunking the end of a slice of pizza into his coffee.

"A regular cast," she assured him.

Jacob sounded suspicious as he asked, "Is he really going to come home tomorrow? Sometimes Dad treats us like we're still little kids so he won't tell us stuff if he thinks we'll worry."

"I mean, they're not planning to amputate his leg or something like that, are they?" Michael added, fishing out a slice of pepperoni that had slid off the cheese into his cup.

"Heavens, no!" Sara set her cup down so suddenly that coffee sloshed onto her fingers. "Of course not." She wiped her wet hand on to her jeans. "He's royally mad about his boots—"

Michael stopped her with a groan. "We heard. We heard *all* about it."

"But other than that he's fine. They said he'd be released right after lunch. I'll run in and pick him up and bring him back here—"

She broke off, frowning at the thought. "Is your dad's bedroom downstairs?"

The boys shook their heads.

"How about that guest room you got ready for me?"

Another simultaneous shake.

"I was just thinking, it's going to be hard for your dad to go up the stairs for a few days. Is there somewhere downstairs we could set up a bed for him?"

"The couch in the office folds out into a bed," Jacob volunteered. "But it sort of sinks in the middle."

"Let's go take a look and see if we can't fix something up." She stood and carried her cup to the sink.

"My turn to do the dishes!" Michael shouted, jumping from his chair. He grabbed the two empty pizza boxes and, with a flourish, stuffed them into the trash can under the sink. "Done!"

Jacob looked daggers, but, in a show of restraint, he turned his back on Michael's smile of triumph. "The office is this way, ma'am," he said formally, obviously trying to appear more mature than his brother.

Once again, Sara found herself hiding a smile as she followed his stiff and dignified back down a hallway to a book-lined room.

The boys tugged and pulled until they had the couch transformed into a bed, albeit with a sizable sag in the center. Still, they decided it was better than the stairs, and after a quick search for sheets and blankets pronounced the office a suitable sickroom ready for Mac's return.

"Anything else you can think of?" Jacob asked, giving the mattress another bounce.

She shook her head. "Looks good to me."

"Then I think I'll head for my room and listen to some tunes." He was at the door in two strides. "Good night, ma'am. Thank you for your help."

Michael looked desperately after his brother, and she knew this was Jacob's revenge for the dishes scam. He'd left Michael alone to entertain her for the rest of the evening, slick as a whistle.

"How about another cup of coffee, Michael?"

"Uh, no thanks. I, uh—" His freckles blended together as his face reddened.

She took pity on him. "I think I'll pour me a cup, then call it a night, if that's all right with you. It's been a long day."

"That would be great. I mean," he amended hastily, "you have all the coffee you want. Or watch some TV or something. I guess I'm going to my room, too, so you can just—"

"You go on up. I'll let myself out."

"Night." He bolted for the stairs as if afraid she'd change her mind and want a partner for an evening of gin rummy or someone to hold her yarn.

She retraced her steps to the kitchen, filled her cup, then unplugged the coffeemaker and dumped the rest of the pot down the sink. Leaning against the counter, she looked around the big, cluttered, old-fashioned kitchen. The refrigerator and stove gleamed white with the rounded edges she remembered from appliances of her childhood. Their heavy lines were at odds with expensive Mexican tile, oak cupboards and a custom countertop that spoke of a recent remodel. One wall was decorated with shining copper molds—a fish, a sun, a pineapple—their soft glow warming the room. She wondered if they were a leftover touch from the days of that ex-wife Mac seemed so reluctant to discuss.

The glass front of a dusty oak china cabinet protected a collection of salt and pepper shakers, an unexpected, whimsical touch. Another legacy of the ex-Mrs. Wallace? But the wide selection of shakers, in the shape of everything from farm animals to windmills, seemed more likely to be the work of one of those Scottish grandmothers of Mac's. Anything that lovingly collected wouldn't have been left behind in a divorce.

She cradled her heavy brown coffee mug between her hands and walked through the arched doorway that led to the living room. A very lived-in living room, she thought. A beige-and-brown-flecked sofa was pushed underneath wide windows, its chocolate brown throw pillows showing the permanent compression of repeated heads. The newspapers on the coffee table had streaked the dust when they'd been shoved aside to make room for a plate that still held the crust of a sandwich. She glanced at the titles of the newspapers and saw the daily from Cheyenne as well as the *Wall Street Journal*. A *Sports Illustrated* curled on the floor next to a dark leather easy chair. A pair of tennis shoes and a hand-held video game sat on top of the television next to a stack of video tapes.

Everything looked well worn, well used, a cheerful masculine clutter—and Sara found her fingers itching to put it straight. The framed landscape on the wall hung slightly off-kilter, the crocheted afghan on the back of the couch needed smoothing, the pillows needed plumping—and Sara *had* to straighten, smooth and plump. She had to make the room perfect. The feeling was so overwhelming, so reminiscent, brought back so many memories, she felt her throat constrict and her heart hammer erratically. Here was what she'd spent the last two years trying to forget.

She was across the room in a flash. She flung open the front door and almost ran to the porch railing, gripping it with white knuckles as she feasted her eyes on the empty, clean, open Wyoming night that surrounded her.

A perfectionist, her husband had labeled her. Greg had loved to psychoanalyze her, and he'd taken great pleasure in pointing out how self-defeating her behavior was. If she hated yard work so much, why did she plant so many flowers every spring? If she hated housework, why did she spend so much time polishing the silverware? And he asked it in that oh-so-reasonable way that set her teeth on edge, watching her over the rim of his glasses with his calm brown eyes. How could she explain that, as much as she hated yard work, she hated weeds more? That, as much as she hated housework, she couldn't stand spots on the glasses or streaks on the windows?

She couldn't explain these things to herself, much less to Greg. All she knew was that she'd spent years cleaning, straightening, weeding, making things perfect for her husband and her daughter. Then one summer day, two years after Greg's death, she'd found herself stretching a plastic cover over her sofa. She'd sat on the cold, clear, crackling plastic that let the creamy floral print show through, seen but not felt, and imagined the day—soon—when unfeeling plastic would cover more and more of her life.

That had been the turning point. She'd put her house on the market the next day. Now she pleased only herself. Now she straightened only her own little world. And if she were being selfish, as Laura accused, if she was only thinking of herself, meeting her own needs—so be it.

Sara looked at the star-filled sky, a brilliant chaos of light and dark. If she was selfish, dammit, she deserved it after more than twenty years of being the perfect wife and mother. She loved her freedom and the new life she'd made for herself. And she wasn't about to let a cowboy hat and incredible midnight blue eyes make her forget all the reasons she'd chosen the life she had. This time tomorrow night she'd be in Yellowstone, and MacKenzie Wallace, his children, his messy living room, his antique salt and pepper shakers, all would join her collection of memories. The only things she ever wanted to own again.

"How much longer?" Mac fumed, shifting irritably in the wheelchair. "When you said after lunch I figured you were talking about this time zone."

"Just hold your horses," Susie said. "One more form

and you'll be on your way. Don't know what your hurry is, anyhow. It's not like you're going to be doin' any dancing."

The nurse looked at Sara, who sat on one of the molded plastic chairs that lined the hospital hallway. "You takin' this man dancing tonight, Sara?"

"I don't think so, Susie. I'm on my way to Yellowstone this afternoon."

"If we ever get out of here," Mac muttered. He put his hands on the wheels of the chair and awkwardly managed to turn himself away from Susie's desk and roll next to Sara. His jeans had been slit to the knee to fit over the cast, and he cradled his ruined elephant-hide boot on his lap, the undamaged boot firmly ensconced on his other foot.

"The boys called this morning and said you fixed them pancakes and eggs for breakfast," he said. "They were pretty impressed."

"I thought they needed a good breakfast considering that list of chores they reeled off for me—feeding horses, changing irrigating tubes, mowing the lawn and having one of them at the station almost round the clock. I was impressed, myself."

"They work hard." The simple statement emphasized Mac's pride in his sons.

"They gave me a guided tour of some of the ranch— that's the first time I've ever been on the back of one of those ATVs. It was quite an experience, I must admit." She paused and frowned, remembering again the impressive size of the small portion of the ranch she'd seen.

"Mac, I was wondering, is there somebody who can give them a hand until you can get around a little better? Six weeks in a cast is a long time. It must be hard to take care of the ranch even when you're all healthy."

"We'll be fine—" he looked over his shoulder in Su-

sie's direction "—if I ever get out of here." He turned to
Sara and grinned, obviously enjoying harassing the nurse.
"Don't worry about us. I'll be back in the saddle in no
time. I've already been practicing on my crutches."

"He's a regular Fred Astaire." Susie heaved herself
from her chair and gathered a stack of papers. She held
them out to Mac. "Here you go. You're a free man."

Sara hopped up and took hold of the handles at the back
of the chair, but Mac already had his hands on the wheels.
"I can do it." He grabbed the papers from Susie as he
passed, pointedly ignoring the small white sack she held,
and began to roll himself down the hall.

Sara looked helplessly at the other woman. Susie sighed
and handed her the sack. "He's going to be begging for
these by the time he gets home. Going to be a lot of pain
for another day or so. Tell the boys to give him one of
these pills every six hours and he'll sleep like a baby."

Sara nodded. "I'll tell them."

"Hold on there a minute, Mac," Susie yelled after him.
"Hospital rules say I have to push you to the curb. You
just slow down." She started after Mac, then stopped and
turned to Sara. "Have the boys call Libby as soon as she
gets home from Cheyenne. They're going to need some
help whether he wants to admit it or not."

"I'll tell them."

"Good luck," she said before huffing after Mac's rapidly departing figure.

Once again Sara was tucked against Mac in the confines
of her truck's cab. His casted foot rested on the same stack
of pillows and his arm was again draped across the back
of her seat. But this time he didn't request her life story
to keep his mind off his pain. He was asleep before they
passed the last T-shirt shop on the outskirts of Dutch
Creek.

She allowed herself to relax and enjoy the warmth of him, the broad masculine angles that provided a natural counterpoint to her feminine curves. He'd shaved and changed into the clean clothes she'd brought him and smelled faintly of the raw, clinical soap the hospital provided. Surreptitiously, moving slowly so as not to jar him, she reached up and angled the rearview mirror so it reflected his face.

She studied him while he slept, watching him more often than the road. She discovered a faint scar on his forehead and a tiny mole just below his ear. His brown hair had a few strands of silver at the temple, and he'd nicked himself shaving the edge of his jaw.

She cherished these details, aware that soon they would be all she would have left of Mac. The drive to the ranch seemed to take mere minutes. She pushed the mirror into position as they approached the little white gas station. She turned by the mailbox, then started up the drive to the house.

"Mac?" she murmured, nudging him with her shoulder.

A low moan was his only response.

"Mac. We're here."

The sudden silence as she turned off the key roused him and he lifted his head from where it rested on the back of the seat, groggy and disoriented. He swore, returning consciousness obviously bringing unwelcome sensations.

"Susie gave me some pain pills. She said you'd need one about now."

"I'll be—"

"I know, I know—you'll be fine."

She got out and went to open Mac's door. The sputter of an engine heralded Michael's approach from the station, and Jacob came at a run from the direction of the corrals beside the barn. Both boys stopped an arm's length from the truck to stare at their father as he sat immobile in the cab, his face a sickly gray.

"He looks worse now than he did yesterday," Michael declared.

"You look awful," Jacob agreed.

"It's good to see you, too. Now help me out of here."

Sara retrieved his crutches from the camper, and Mac used them to support himself as he lowered his feet to the ground. He swayed and swallowed so hard it was audible. Three sets of hands reached out to steady him, but he waved them off.

"Just a little dizzy." Moving awkwardly on the crutches, he made his way up the porch stairs and into the house. Sara and the boys hovered mere inches away.

"Mac, you really do look bad," she said, unable to stand it any longer. "Let's get you to bed and—"

"I'm fine, dammit, I—" He stopped. As she watched in dismay, Mac's pallor deteriorated from gray to a pasty shade of green. Moving with a speed she wouldn't have thought possible on crutches, he pivoted and swung down the hallway, ducking into the bathroom and slamming the door behind him.

She waited, the boys silent and young and worried beside her, until the door opened and Mac reappeared, wiping his mouth with the back of his hand.

"I think I'll lay down for a minute after all," he said. Slowly, but with a face determinedly grim, he started for the stairs.

She stopped him. "We made up the couch in the office. We thought it would be easier."

"Good idea." With no mention of the sag he must have known existed, he made his way to the room at the end of the hall and sank onto the waiting clean sheets with a sigh.

Jacob took the crutches from him and leaned them against the wall. Michael carefully lifted his casted foot and rested it on a plump pillow. Sara opened the little sack and shook out a pill from the amber-colored bottle. She poured a glass of water from the pitcher waiting on the desk and held both water and pill out to him.

"Damned things knock me out," Mac complained, but he took the pill and a swallow of water without further protest.

Sara and the boys stood on each side of the bed, looking on him as he lay in the middle of the room. Mac closed his eyes. No one moved. The boys seemed as reluctant to leave as she felt. Finally, Mac opened one eye and peered at Michael.

"Who's watching the station?"

"Uh, I locked off the pumps and put that Back in Five Minutes sign on the door," Michael replied.

"It's been five minutes."

"Yes, sir."

Mac opened his other eye and lifted his head slightly off the pillow. "Jacob, did you change the dressing on that calf this morning? The one with the wire cut?"

"Not yet."

"It's long past morning."

"Yes, sir."

Mac lay down. No one moved.

"You going to spend all day staring at me?" His sudden bark made Sara jump as high as the boys. "There's work to be done." He waved his hand in the direction of his crutches. "Move those things over here next to the bed. I'm going to take a little nap then I'll be up in a half hour to check on that calf. Go on, get going."

Michael and Jacob smiled broadly and, reassured, left the room.

"I thought I was going to have to pry them out of here with a crowbar," he said to her.

"They've been worried about you."

"Well, I'm home now and things will be back to normal in no time."

She didn't believe him for a minute but made no comment as she retrieved the crutches from against the wall and set them alongside the bed. Then she busied herself placing the water pitcher and glass within easy reach on the desk, moving the bottle of pain pills a few inches closer, quick little gestures she knew betrayed her nervousness. Once again, it was time to say goodbye.

Mac watched her, saying nothing, until she ran out of things to straighten and stood beside him.

"I guess you're ready to go, then?"

She nodded. "I had Michael write me up a repair bill this morning, so that's all taken care of." She smoothed her hand over her ponytail and tucked a stray piece of hair behind one ear.

"Good. Well, have a nice time in Yellowstone—or wherever you finally end up in that big circle you're making." He gave a huge yawn. "Uh-oh, it looks like those white bombs are kicking in."

"I better go. Let you get your rest. I'll—"

"Sara?"

She stopped and looked at the hand Mac stretched out to her. Taking a step closer to the bed, she slowly slipped her hand inside his.

"Thank you," he said.

"You're welcome."

His eyes closed, his breaths lengthened, and still he held her hand. She let it remain cradled in his for a moment longer, savoring the warmth, adding the feeling to her precious collection of memories. Then she laid his hand on his chest and let her fingers drift whisper-soft from his. She walked quietly toward the door.

"Don't feed the bears," she heard him murmur as she pulled the door shut behind her.

* * *

Sara strode through the living room, trying to ignore the plate with the half-eaten sandwich that still decorated the coffee table. Not her house, not her dishes, not her life, she reminded herself sternly. She was on her way to the Grand Tetons. A quiet moment alone with a man and she went all soft and dewy inside, she thought in disgust, wanting to shake the disturbing feelings Mac had aroused. She wiped the hand he had held on her jeans, trying to stop the strange throb that remained from his touch. Not her man, not her cowboy, not her problem.

She was almost running by the time she got to her camper, but came to an abrupt stop as she found Jacob waiting for her, leaning against the fender well, hands tucked in the back pockets of his jeans with studied nonchalance.

"How's the calf?" she asked.

"The vet's coming tomorrow morning to take a look at him but I think he'll be fine." Jacob patted the side of her camper. "It must be pretty cool to travel around seeing all kinds of places like you do."

She smiled. "You meet some interesting people."

"You probably don't like staying in one place too long, huh?" Jacob kicked at one of the tires with his boot, not meeting her eyes. "I mean, like, you wouldn't want to stay here another night. You probably want to keep moving?"

"Sometimes I'll stay in one spot a few days," she answered carefully. "Once I even spent a month in this little town near Tucson."

"It would probably have to be a really great place, though, huh? I mean, you wouldn't want to stay in a place like this."

She looked around her, at the cedar fence posts of the corrals, the dark green fields of alfalfa, the rangeland that went on and on, nothing stopping her gaze until the Grand

Tetons, whose majestic peaks were no more than a smudge
on the horizon. It was beautiful, in a stark sort of way.
The cottonwoods around the house and outbuildings provided shade and a pleasant rustle as the wind glided
through their broad leaves. The sky was the intense blue
that only the West could paint, with sunshine as thick and
heavy as syrup.

She wouldn't mind at all spending a few days in such
a laconic setting, but what was Jacob really asking? "I've
always liked this part of the country. Oh, I forgot to tell
you," she added with what she hoped was a casual air,
"the nurse at the hospital told me to tell you to call Libby
when she gets back. I take it Libby's a friend of yours?"

Jacob nodded. "Her parents own the next ranch. Libby
and her daughter just moved back home last month to help
take care of them 'cause they're getting really old. The
parents are getting old, I mean, not Libby."

"Oh."

"The trouble is, Libby won't be home until Monday."
Jacob almost wailed the words. The miserable look on his
face left her in no doubt that, indeed, he'd been hinting
for her to stay.

"I can handle the chores fine and I can cook supper
okay," he went on. "We can have burritos for a couple
of nights, I guess, and Michael will do what I tell him
most of the time, but—"

"But there's the laundry and the dishes," she guessed.

"And the lawn *really* needs mowing. I'm thinking of
letting the goat in to have a go at it."

She sighed. That blasted sandwich crust on the coffee
table was bothering her no end. Could she really just drive
away?

It had been a good long while since Mac had had a
hangover, but he remembered the gluey tongue, the gravel

under the eyelids, the pain at the base of the skull. He hoped to hell he'd had a good time.

He opened his eyes carefully and squinted at the clock through sunlight that flooded the room with the subtlety of a jackhammer. Eleven-thirty. He started to roll over, to bury his head in the pillow until the sun dimmed a little, but the heavy weight on his leg brought him up short. His eyes grated open and he jerked upright, only to be slammed down by a pain that shot from toes to chest. Memory returned with the pain and Mac lay still, cocooned in the sagging mattress, while he waited for the ache to subside.

He was relieved when it dulled to a manageable level. Not nearly so bad as when he'd laid down yesterday. Yesterday! He glared at the clock again as if by force of will alone he could make it repudiate the fact that he'd slept almost twenty-four hours. Dammit! He struggled to a sitting position, stubbornly ignoring the pain. The boys must be frantic—the place must be a shambles—all the chores— Why hadn't somebody woken him!

He swung his good leg to the floor and used both hands to slowly lower his casted foot to join it. Pins and needles raced up and down his skin. He reached for his boot on the floor next to the bed, although he didn't remember putting it there, and tugged it on. Using the crutches, he slowly raised himself, then awkwardly tucked his shirttail into his jeans while he waited for the dizziness to recede. The room spun and black honeycombs swam before his eyes, but he shook them off.

He knew the boys were pretty self-sufficient—growing up on an isolated ranch, they had to be—but they must be getting worried by now. He should have been up yesterday afternoon, taking care of business, not lying in bed in a drugged coma. Damned pills, anyway. He picked up the small bottle from the desk, still full of white tablets.

He turned the bottle over and over, listening to the pills rattle against each other. He remembered Sara holding one out to him, her eyes full of warmth and concern. He remembered the feel of her hand in his, soft and tiny, comforting, as he sank into the thickening haze of pain and medication. She was in Yellowstone by now, alone in her tidy, possession-free camper. And he missed her. He allowed himself the luxury of missing Sara for a moment, knowing that a moment was all they'd shared. Just a brief moment in time.

He tossed the bottle in the trash can next to the desk and, grasping the crutches firmly, made his way to the door.

Mac was pleasantly surprised to see how great the living room looked as he swung through it toward the kitchen. He'd thought those tennis shoes were going to be a permanent fixture on the television. The stack of newspapers was gone from the coffee table and it even looked as if the boys had dusted. He sniffed at the faint scent of lemon polish.

The kitchen was another surprise. There was no mess from supper last night, although he knew they must have foraged for themselves. The place was spotless. Way too clean, he realized with a frown. He was proud of the way the boys had pitched in and taken care of the house, but if the house was this clean, then they must have let some of the outside chores slip. There was no way they could do both.

As he started for the back door, his crutches slipping on the tile floor, he heard the sound of the lawn mower start up. No, no, he thought, Jacob should be getting the water on the hay and let the lawn go—even if it was so long you could almost cut and bale it for feed. He shoved open the screen door with his shoulder and ducked through before it swung closed. Standing on the porch, he heard the sound of the mower come closer, the fragrant smell of cut grass filling the air.

Dressed in cutoffs and a white T-shirt, Sara pushed the red-under-the-rust machine around the corner of the house. She stopped when she saw him and gave him a tentative smile, eyes as wide as a startled doe in a meadow.

Mac found himself returning the smile. He was glad—fiercely glad—that their moment was going to last just a little while longer.

Chapter Four

Sara leaned over and turned the knob that cut the mower's
engine. She straightened and wiped her hands nervously
on her shorts. A bird shrilled from the lilac bush near the
corner of the house, loud and raucous in the sudden silence.

"Hi," she said.

Mac didn't respond. His first brief smile had faded, and
she couldn't read the odd look in his eyes. He asked,
"Where are the boys?"

"Michael's at the station and Jacob said something
about irrigating the alfalfa." She rested a hand on the
mower and added unnecessarily, "I'm, uh, mowing the
lawn." What was he thinking? she wondered a bit wildly,
feeling awkward and self-conscious. That he didn't seem
to be able to get rid of her? That, in spite of Cyrus's rec-
ommendation, she was some crazy stalker? That she didn't
understand goodbye?

She looked at him as he stood on the porch, his expression still inscrutable. His hair had been raked back from

his forehead by hurried fingers, his shirt was wrinkled from hours of sleep, his jaw was stubbled with a dark, overnight growth—and Sara thought he looked rumpled, the slightest bit vulnerable, and incredibly sexy.

He said, "I thought you and your camera would be waiting for Old Faithful to blow right about now."

"I thought so, too. But—"

"All right! Sleeping Beauty finally got his butt out of bed!" Jacob came around the corner of the house, a muddy shovel in one hand, rubber boots squishing on his feet. He grinned at his father. "Isn't it great that Sara said she'd stay for a couple days? I had to beg, of course, but all it took was the thought of Mike's tuna slop surprise for supper and I got down on my knees—quick."

"That would do it," Mac agreed, his voice mild. "Did you get the water on the hay?"

"I'm a few tubes short. I'll be finished in half an hour."

"The stalls?"

"Clean as a whistle."

Mac nodded. "Good job."

Jacob's beaming smile as he headed in the direction of the barn told Sara this was high praise.

Mac watched his son's departing figure for a moment then turned to her. "It sounds like you were shang-haied—blackmailed by tuna surprise into staying the night."

"I was willing." She walked across the grass and climbed the porch stairs to perch on the edge of a white wicker love seat. "The boys seemed a little overwhelmed yesterday. I told them I'd be glad to help out until your neighbors get back. Maybe—Libby?—might be able to give you a hand then."

"Trouble is, Libby's got her own plate full taking care of her daughter, her folks and their ranch." He swung across the porch to join her, and the wicker creaked under his weight. He let the crutches drop to the wooden planks. "But me and the boys won't really need any more help. We'll get by fine on our own now that I'm up and around. We can't ask you to drop everything and stay here."

"I don't exactly have a full social calendar right now," she said in a dry voice. "I've got a dentist appointment in Denver right after Labor Day, but that leaves me a few free hours between now and then." She tucked her hands between her knees and leaned forward earnestly. "Look, Mac, this whole accident is my fault anyway." She stopped his immediate protest. "Even if it isn't, it feels like it is. It was my truck, my problems that got you into this mess. The least I can do is take care of a little cooking and cleaning for a couple days to get you over the rough spots."

Mac sighed and looked at his cast, wiggling his toes experimentally. "It looks like the spots are going to be rougher than I thought."

Her sharp glance saw his skin was still pale under the stubble of beard. "Do you need another pain pill?"

"I threw them out."

"Mac!"

"I can't sleep all day! I've got a ranch to run."

She glared at him and frowned, impatient at his stubbornness. "You're not going to be running anything or anywhere for quite a while so you might as well get used to accepting help—accepting it *graciously*, I might add."

Mac's brow was as furrowed as hers, and he matched her glare. "Would you be offended if I offered to pay you?"

Her lips quirked. "Mildly. Although I wouldn't say no to an offer of a bath."

Her smile froze at the look that flamed in his eyes. She felt seared from top to bottom as an unfamiliar heat raced through her. It pooled in the pit of her stomach and dropped lower, thick and heavy. She shifted, glad when the wicker scraped painfully against the back of her thighs. His body, only inches from her on the love seat, seemed unbearably close—unbearably male.

"I—I mean, a bathtub," she stuttered. "After a few months in a camper, a real bathtub is worth its weight in gold."

The flame lowered to a slower, lazier warmth, just as dangerous and infinitely attractive, as he said, "I can do one better than that. I can offer you an entire remodeled guest bedroom and throw in an attached bathroom for free."

She shied away from the implied intimacy of sleeping under the same roof, immediately shaking her head. "I'll sleep in the camper. It's all set up just the way I like it, and that way I won't be imposing—"

"What was it you were saying about accepting offers *graciously?*"

He had her there. "All right. The guest bedroom it is." Eager to get on a more impersonal footing, she made her voice brisk as she told him, "Speaking of bed, you should be getting back in one."

"I just got up!"

"And how do you feel?"

"Fine," he said with a defiant lift of his chin. "Fine and dandy."

"Liar."

He laughed, then conceded, "Maybe a little wobbly."

"You need some food in you." She stood and gathered his crutches from the floor with efficient movements, much more comfortable when Mac was relegated to the role of patient. "Why don't you lie down and I'll bring you some soup."

"I need a shower first."

She nodded. "Then bed."

"All right, already." He took the crutches from her and pulled himself to his feet, muttering, "Never met a woman in such a hurry to get me in bed before."

Sara laughed and refused to blush as she followed him into the house. What could it hurt? she asked herself as she handed him a plastic garbage bag to protect his cast and watched him head down the hallway to the bathroom. A day or two spent skittering along the edge of a dangerous attraction—surely, she was safe. She hadn't felt the least interest in a man in years. A little mild flirtation was harmless, maybe even a good thing, a way to keep her from drying up and blowing away like the crushed leaves under her tires. Mac Wallace posed no threat to her way of life. On Tuesday—or maybe Wednesday—she'd just drive away.

Sara heard the shower shut off as she ladled soup into a bowl. She set the bowl on a tray she'd found in a cupboard above the refrigerator and carried it into the office. Mac had changed his shirt, but was wearing the same pair of slit jeans as he sat propped in bed, his cast resting on a stack of pillows. His hair curled damply around his ears and the clean smell of after-shave weaved around the aroma of the soup, making her want to breathe deeply the normal, everyday smells of other people's lives.

"It sure feels a lot better when it's up," Mac told her, pointing to his foot.

"Give it time. It's hardly been forty-eight hours since you broke it."

"Seems longer."

It did to her, too. She settled the tray over his lap and watched while he dug hungrily into the vegetable soup. She'd started it simmering that morning, knowing he would need something light when he finally woke up.

"This is great," he said, and she was unaccountably pleased. It had been four years since she'd cooked for a man, almost that long since she'd cooked for anybody. When she visited her mother or Laura in Denver, they liked to cook for her—her mother to baby her with childhood favorites and her daughter to impress her with tofu and tiramisu. But Mac ate her soup with the same flattering gusto the boys had shown her spaghetti last night.

Of course, the man hadn't eaten in a day, she thought dryly, and the house special at Chez Wallace was something called tuna slop surprise. She shouldn't be too impressed with the enthusiasm they showed her cooking. Besides, she reminded herself, she'd always hated to cook. It was repetitive, messy, time-consuming and almost always taken for granted.

"I better finish the lawn," she told him, suddenly eager for fresh air and movement. The office was a small room to begin with, and the sofa-bed took up most of it. Mac's presence overwhelmed the confined space. She felt uneasy with the way he dominated the room, dominated her thoughts, her senses.

"The vet's supposed to stop by today. Let me know when he gets here and I'll go take a look at that calf's leg with him."

"He came this morning after church. Jacob talked to him."

"Oh." Mac seemed disconcerted, whether at the realization that he'd slept through such a large chunk of time or that things had gone so smoothly without him, she couldn't tell. "Well, roll that computer table over here, please, and I'll take care of some paperwork as long as I'm just sitting here." He pointed to a small, wheeled table with a computer, printer and stack of manila folders on top.

"Let me go turn off the soup first," she hedged, knowing work was the last thing Mac should be doing. "I'll be right back." She dawdled in the kitchen for a few minutes fixing sandwiches for the boys, and when she returned to the office, sure enough, Mac was sound asleep, the tray with the empty bowl of soup on the floor beside the bed.

Her lips curved into a gentle smile as she picked up a blanket from the foot of the bed to cover him. Her fingers brushed lightly against his chest as she settled the blanket around him, and a guilty thrill of pleasure swept over her. Unable to help herself, she smoothed the blanket, trailing her fingers over its fluffy softness, reveling in the contrast of the hard bulk of his chest and arms underneath.

The slam of the screen door made her start. She snatched back her hand and hastily bent to pick up the tray, hurrying out of the room to greet Jacob as he returned from the fields.

After settling the boy at the table in front of soup and a plate of sandwiches, she walked down the long drive to the station by the highway. Michael gave her a quick lesson in how to run the cash register before heading to the house for his lunch.

Within minutes, Sara had a bottle of cleanser and a rag in her hand and was cleaning the station's bathroom, telling herself a clean bathroom was so important when you were on the road. Later, after she finished mowing the lawn, she told herself how necessary it was to catch the weeds in the garden while they were still small, before they took over the corn and smothered the tomatoes. And after she'd scrubbed the dirt from under her fingernails, she reminded herself to start the roast early so she'd have plenty of time to make the gravy and rolls.

By four o'clock that afternoon, she was peeling carrots to add to the roast in a pan on the counter. The scraper snicked against the thin skin, unwinding a long orange curl with each deft flick of her wrist. Suddenly her hands stilled, the staccato rhythm broken, and she let a carrot slide from her fingers to join the peels in the bottom of the deep kitchen sink. She stood very still, motionless for the first time in hours, as she realized, with a start, that she was humming. Humming? Good lord, she was almost ready to burst into song!

She was *enjoying* this, she thought in dismay. But she *hated* to cook, and she hated housework, and yard work, and laundry, and cleaning. In fact, she hated all the things she'd spent the entire day doing. Quickly, she gathered up the vegetables, chunked them and slid the roast into the oven, her mind racing. Playing house, she decided, letting the oven door slam shut. That's all it was. All those things, done day after day, became tedious chores, but doing them once every few years relegated them to a game—just like playing house. When you didn't *have* to do them, they were sort of fun.

She clamped her lips on the little ditty that skipped joyfully around inside her head. She made herself take a hard look at the kitchen around her. She forced herself to imagine wiping down the stove three times a day, day after day, scrubbing those little splatters of spaghetti sauce off the tiles behind it every other Thursday, year after year. She stared at the sunny yellow curtains stretched across the window over the sink, looking past their cheerful color to the reality that they needed a good washing and ironing. She reminded herself the refrigerator shelves had something sticky on them, like a can of soda had tipped over. And the homey braided rug by the back door could use a good shake. A couple of shirts she'd folded that morning had buttons missing, and Michael was due for a haircut—

The song in her head screeched to a halt, like a needle against a record. Never again! She'd promised herself two years ago that she'd never face a list like that again. A never-ending, never-changing list of things to be set right before she could rest. She'd ripped herself from that life at great personal anguish and she'd never go back. She liked to travel, to lose herself in a good book, to take long walks through quiet woods, to breathe in and out to her own rhythm—that was her life now.

Resolute, she threw the peelings into the trash, rinsed out the sink and wiped off the counter. Then she went upstairs to Mac's bedroom and opened dresser drawers until she found his jeans. Retrieving her sewing kit from her camper, she sat in the wicker love seat on the porch, a pair of Mac's jeans on her lap, and began to rip the outside seam from ankle to knee.

The repetitive movement calmed her, a shaft of sun warmed her back, a breeze, still scented with newly mown grass, tickled her nose. As her fingers worked, she felt the heavy laziness of a summer afternoon settle around her. The melody crept back, slipping sideways through an unguarded crack in her subconscious, to begin its cautious dance. And Sara felt deliciously, dangerously, frighteningly content.

"That smells great," Mac said, entering the kitchen as Sara bent over the open oven to remove a roast. "I'm starving." He was hungry, he realized, and he relished the sensation. The last of the medication had worked its way through his system, and although his ankle still throbbed, the clean, distinct pain was better than the muzzy haze he'd been in since the accident. He felt strong and healthy—and hungry.

"I think it turned out pretty good," Sara said as she set the roast on the stove top. "It's been a while since I've cooked something this big, but it looks like I haven't lost my touch." She pulled off the oven mitts and turned to face him. "Hey, you're looking good! How's the leg?"

"Good as new." He thought she was the one looking good. Her black denims fit the way a man's pants were meant to fit a woman, straining across her hips and hugging her bottom like cupped hands. Her white, short-sleeved shirt was decorated with tiny sprigs of flowers, like one of his grandmother's old teacups. She'd gathered up her brown hair in some kind of loose swirl on top of her head, held in place with a gold clasp, tiny wisps trailing across the back of her neck and around her ears. Her cheeks were flushed, whether from the heat of the oven or the heat of his scrutiny, he didn't know. But she looked beautiful, delicate, patrician—and too damn classy for his kitchen.

He pulled out a chair from the table and sat down, leaning his crutches against the table. The crutches started to slide, and Sara reached to grab them at the same time he did. His hand wrapped around hers on the smooth wood and their arms entangled as they juggled the awkward crutches, managing to stop them before they fell.

Sara froze, half bent over him, her face close to his, her lips parted. Her eyes flew to his, startled and wary, their gray as elusive as smoke. Moving slowly, his eyes never leaving her face, Mac took the crutches from her and laid them carefully on the floor.

"I can see this is going to be a hell of an inconvenience," he said softly, sure he was talking only about the crutches.

Sara was the first to break the spell. She blinked and straightened, then gave him a small, confused smile before she turned to the stove to begin making gravy.

He felt confused himself. His kitchen was full of the womanly aromas of spices and home-cooked food, womanly touches like floral oven mitts instead of the dish towel he and the boys usually grabbed to pull a pan from the oven, womanly sights like a table set with the good dishes and cloth napkins. They usually didn't bother to set the table, since taking a plate from the cupboard and dishing straight from the stove saved washing all those serving bowls. It had been a long time since he'd had a woman in his kitchen, and he allowed himself a brief moment to enjoy the differences. But only a brief moment. Those sights, smells and feminine touches were the past. It was just him and the boys now.

Which didn't mean he couldn't enjoy the yeasty smell of the rolls Sara slid into the oven—or the sight of those black denims as she bent over. He managed to drag his eyes from the curve of her pants as she moved to the counter to slice the roast, thick slabs of meat, reddened juice oozing onto the cutting board with each pass of the knife. His stomach rumbled.

Sara laughed at the sound. "I heard that. It's nice to be appreciated."

"It's nice to have a meal to appreciate. It's not like we live on TV dinners or anything, but meals are usually pretty basic around here."

"Meat and potatoes, huh?"

"Sometimes not even the potato part—just slap a steak on the grill and call it a night."

"Bad for your arteries." She slid the sliced meat onto a platter.

He shrugged. "We pared things down to the bare necessities after the divorce."

She looked at him over her shoulder. "And vegetables weren't considered a necessity?"

"Not at first. Not vegetables, or serving bowls, matching socks, clean sheets, good-night kisses—" He heard his voice deepen with bitterness as the list went on, and he forced himself to stop.

Sara carried the platter to the table. "It must have been hard on the boys." Her eyes added, *And on you, too*, but he was glad she didn't say it.

He picked up a fork and traced patterns with its tines

on the tablecloth he'd forgotten he owned. "It took us awhile, but we managed to get our priorities straight."

"How long ago was the divorce?"

"Five years." He was sorry he'd mentioned it. She stood next to his chair, full of warmth and concern. He knew women loved to delve into broken relationships, ready to comfort and empathize and examine every facet. He was going to end up answering a string of questions.

Sure enough, Sara asked, "Do the boys see their mother much?"

"All the time. It's not as if Ronda deserted them. They were old enough to decide for themselves that they didn't want to live in an apartment in Cheyenne. It was all very amicable. They spend lots of weekends with her, school vacations, a few weeks in the summer— Ronda's a good mother, all things considered." He was pleased he'd managed to add that last part. Made him sound magnanimous and well-adjusted.

But Sara frowned, evidently still bothered, and said, "It must have been so hard for her to leave the boys."

"Obviously not as hard as it was to stay." The bitterness was back, and Mac hated it. He clamped his mouth shut.

Sara didn't seem to know how to respond, but she remained by the table, patient, waiting for him to continue. Mac sighed, resigned. Him and his big mouth. But it was too late to back out now. He'd give her the edited version of Ronda's decision to leave him, he decided, the version Ronda had told him. The version he'd believed before he'd found out the truth.

He dropped the fork onto the table. "It's not that unusual a story. I know other couples it's happened to. Ronda was raised on a ranch just outside of Dutch Creek. She knew all about being a rancher's wife when we got married. But, bit by bit, she just got worn down by everything.

She said she was tired of the isolation, the hard work, the marriage—''

He shrugged, stopping before he got any closer to the truth he never let himself think about. Sara laid a hand on his shoulder. But the warmth of her hand had barely soaked through his shirt to his skin when the timer chimed, signaling the rolls were ready to take out of the oven. Her hand slid away and she went back to work. Like Ronda had said as she'd driven away, tears rolling down her cheeks—the work never stopped.

The house was dark and quiet. The boys had disappeared into their rooms shortly after supper, and Mac had returned to the office, this time to work on the stack of files next to the computer rather than to sleep. He'd been moody and quiet after their talk of divorce, and Sara had left him to his work. She'd moved her few personal items from the camper into a bedroom on the second floor, a high-ceilinged room with decorative molding and floral print wallpaper preserving the turn-of-the-century feel in spite of the modern Berber carpet and sparkling tiled bathroom.

The bed was large and full of plump pillows, and the white chenille bedspread was the perfect weight for a summer night. But she couldn't sleep. She'd tried it with the window open, letting in a breeze still warm from the last of the sun. She'd tried it with the window closed, shutting out the cacophony of crickets. She'd tried reading, listening to her favorite CD and had finally resorted to pacing.

She didn't have the luxury of pacing in the confines of her camper. But that very luxury was probably why she couldn't sleep now, she decided. Everything was too large—the ceiling too far away, the windows enormous, gaping holes, the door unreachable across acres of beige Berber. The damn room would probably echo if she yodeled, she thought irritably, missing the safety of the metal shell never more than an arm's length away. The room made her feel small and a little lost—and unutterably alone.

The plain white T-shirt she wore as a nightshirt came almost to her knees, one of Greg's, thin and soft after many washings. She didn't bother putting anything over it as she made her way down the stairs, across the living room and out the front door to the porch. The night, vast as only a western night could be, surrounded her, its emptiness quixotically comforting. She leaned against the porch rail and took a deep breath, feeling herself relax.

She didn't start at the sound of creaking wicker. Slowly, she turned to pick out Mac's figure in the dim moonlight, seated on the love seat, his casted foot stretched out on a stool in front of him.

"You should be resting," she said, her voice low, soft, not wanting to disturb the peace.

"I've slept for two days straight. I'm not tired." His voice was as quiet as hers. "Can't you sleep?"

She shook her head, although she doubted he could see the motion in the dark. "Strange bed."

"Oh. Well, I appreciate the company. Come have a seat."

Sara crossed the porch and sat next to him. Sensation rippled along her skin—Mac's shoulder brushing against hers as he laid his arm across the back of the seat, the scratchy wicker, the floorboards cool and hard under her bare feet. The combination of textures was strangely erotic, and she shivered.

"You'd think after all that work you did today you'd be dead tired," he said. "Michael told me you even weeded the garden."

"It was sort of fun, really," she admitted, "as a change of pace."

He gave a small laugh. "You need to get out of that truck more often if pulling weeds is your idea of fun." He reached down, picked up a long-necked bottle from the floor and took a swallow. "So, how do you usually spend your day on the road," he asked, "without stuff like weeding to do?"

She could smell the yeasty beer mix with the night odors of dew and cooling earth. She breathed deeply, then let the air out in a slow stream, considering his question. "On a usual day...I drive."

"And?"

"And I look." She shrugged and felt her nightshirt snag on the rough back of the love seat. "And I watch what goes by."

"But don't you ever want to stop and get out?" He waved the bottle for emphasis and its dark glass caught the moonlight. "Every once in awhile, don't you need to get your land legs under you again? Get your hands in the dirt again?"

"No."

"But—"

"Mac, I don't want to get my hands dirty anymore. I don't want to get that close anymore—to *experience* life. Been there, done that, as they say."

He was silent for a moment. She heard the tap as he set the beer bottle on the wooden planks. "Don't you ever wonder what you're missing?"

"Weeds," she said shortly. "I'm missing weeds."

His teeth flashed briefly as he smiled at her emphatic statement. "There's more out here than weeds, and you know it."

She felt him shift beside her, turning to study her, and she wondered how much he saw in the faint light. Could he see the rapid pulse fluttering in her throat, the hard buds of her nipples against her cotton nightshirt, the goose bumps on her skin? She shivered again.

"Cold?" he asked, noticing the ripple of movement.

She shook her head. "Not really."

"Nervous?"

"No!" She looked at him sharply, but his eyes were no more than black pools in the shadow of his face. "Of course not."

"Alone in the dark—with me—in your nightgown. Thought you might be nervous, that's all." His voice rumbled, smooth and deep, like a well-tuned engine.

She made a weak attempt at a laugh, disconcerted at how close he'd come to the truth. "I think I'm safe. After all, I can outrun you."

"If you wanted to run."

"It's what I do best, remember?"

His hand brushed a strand of hair from her cheek, an idle gesture that made her jump nonetheless. If he noticed, he said nothing, instead asking, "Don't you ever get tired of all that running?"

"You just told me you weren't tired because you'd slept for two days."

"So?" His fingers continued to comb through the ends of her hair.

"Well, I slept for over twenty years." She pulled her head away from the caressing movement and stood. "I can run for a long, long time yet."

With a murmured good-night, she walked to the front door slowly, serene and composed—but once the screen door had closed quietly behind her, she ran for the stairs, pounding up them with the same desperate need to escape she'd felt that summer day she'd first driven away from Denver.

Mac heard her feet taking the stairs two at a time. It was a good thing she'd run—before he'd buried his hands in her hair and pulled her to him. Before he'd pressed her breasts, their shape clearly outlined by the thin material of that ridiculous man's T-shirt she wore, against his chest. Before he'd plundered her mouth with a thoroughness that would make her forget she was in such a damned hurry to leave.

He cursed the cast that kept him pinned to the love seat like a helpless moth when what he needed was to pace until the image of Sara standing outlined by moonlight faded along with his restlessness. Until the heady scent of old-fashioned roses that clung to her skin was replaced by the smell of sage and rangeland—things that belonged in his life.

He must be careful, very, very careful, he warned himself. Ronda had taught him a painful lesson he wasn't soon to forget. The last thing he needed was to be attracted to a woman just like her. In spite of the way Sara had helped him out, she'd already proven she was the type to run away from her problems, to bolt when the going got really tough. Her very life-style made her a poster child for mid-life crises. What he needed was a team player for his ranch and his sons, he reminded himself. Definitely not a woman like Sara.

Chapter Five

After two years, Sara's internal rhythms moved more in sync with the unmarked but steady passage of the sun rather than the painstaking precision of the clock. She tended to wake with the first, exploratory rays of light and start to yawn shortly after she was no longer able to see the pages of her book.

But in spite of the early hour as she made her way downstairs Monday morning, the kitchen was already full. Michael dropped frozen waffles into the toaster and Jacob gave a pan of scrambled eggs one last stir. Mac sat at the table, a cup of coffee in front of him, punching figures into a calculator, then scribbling quickly on a form.

"You want 'em scrambled or over easy?" Jacob asked at the sound of her footsteps.

"Scrambled is fine," she told him, walking across the kitchen to peer over his shoulder, "but cooking's supposed to be my job."

"Don't worry, lunch and supper are all yours. Grab some plates. It's time to dish up."

"Mornin'," Mac said. He looked up from his work and smiled at her, and Sara's stomach did an odd little flip-flop in response. "Thanks for the pants. I thought I was going to have to get out my pocket knife and do a little alteration myself."

"You're welcome," she said. She reached into the cupboard and got down four plates. "I hope three pair of jeans will be enough. I didn't want to do too many since somebody's going to have to sew them up again after the cast comes off."

And that somebody isn't going to be me, her words implied. She hadn't meant it to come out like that, but a quick glance at Mac confirmed he'd noticed.

She set the plates on the counter, flustered, and Jacob expertly divided the eggs onto them. Michael added a waffle to each one then carried the plates to the table. Sara grabbed a handful of knives and forks from the drawer next to the sink, milk from the refrigerator and a coffee cup for herself. Everyone was seated and taking a first bite quicker than she would have thought possible.

Mac continued to write even as he ate, not looking in her direction. "Done," he said finally, pushing the papers toward Jacob. "After you stock the shelves, I want you to call in this order. Michael will relieve you at noon."

Jacob nodded. He hopped up from the table, folded the papers and stuffed them into the back pocket of his jeans. He took his plate and still full glass of milk with him and started for the door, drinking as he walked. The empty glass and plate skidded on the counter as he slammed out the screen door for the station.

"Chickens fed?" Mac asked Michael, still lining out the morning's chores.

The boy nodded. "That gray hen, the fat one, she's got herself a nest on the tractor seat. Found three eggs there this morning."

"They'll all be roosting there if I don't get that tire changed. I better plan on doing that today."

"You want me to take that calf to the herd? The vet said he was ready to go."

"I'll do it." Mac reached for his crutches. "I'll go stir-crazy if I don't get out of the house for awhile. Saddle up Justice for me and I'll meet you by the stables in a few minutes."

"Mac, do you really think you should—"

"Can you ride?" he interrupted, intent on his rapid-fire orders.

"Uh, it's been a few years, but I can usually manage to stay in the saddle."

"Hey, Michael," he yelled after the boy who was already bounding down the steps. "Get Patches ready, too." To her he said, "Get on some boots—a pair of Michael's should fit you—and I'll show you the ranch. Don't forget a hat."

"But the dishes—"

"Will be here when we get back, believe me. Come on."

Sara had never left dirty dishes in the sink in her life. That was definitely not right. The kitchen must be put in order after every meal. *That* was right. "But—"

Mac didn't hear her last, feeble attempt at protest. He'd plucked his hat from the top of the refrigerator and was already following Michael to the stables, pulling down the brim against the sun that just breached the horizon.

She stood for a moment in the middle of the kitchen, torn. The plastic syrup bottle sat on the table, coated with sticky brown drips, the butter beside it, softening by the minute. The toaster was still on the counter, decorated with crumbs. The egg pan remained on a stove burner, a lacy ring of egg white around its edge.

A horse's whinny galvanized her to action. She threw

the butter in the refrigerator and the syrup into the cupboard and wiped the table in under a minute flat. Tossing the rag into the sink, she turned her back on the rest and scurried upstairs to change her tennis shoes for boots with a heel that would grab a stirrup. She tugged a baseball cap on her head, pulled her ponytail through the space in the back, then shrugged a windbreaker on over her T-shirt as she ran down the stairs and outside, zipping it up against the morning chill.

Mac was fitting a bridle into the mouth of the big black gelding she'd first seen him on, leaning against the horse's neck for support since his crutches were discarded in the dirt nearby. Michael was spreading a blanket over the back of a little paint mare.

"Here, let me do that," she said, hurrying to Michael. "You help your father." She lifted the waiting saddle onto the mare's back, and her fingers remembered the complicated sequence that followed. She could almost feel her father's big hands over hers, guiding her as she tightened the cinch and adjusted the stirrups to fit her shorter legs. As she worked, she forgot all about dirty dishes in the sink and crumbs on the counter.

Her hand stroked the shiny oiled leather of the saddle and the mare's coarse black-and-white hair with equal reverence, memories bubbling up of summer mornings long ago. The smells were the same, dew and straw and dust and horse. The sounds were the same, leather creaking and hooves shuffling through the dirt as the restless animals twitched and sent ripples skittering along their ready muscles. And the anticipation was the same, that eagerness to swing into the saddle, gather up the reins and run and run and run—

A curse brought her up short. She looked over at the two men and saw the consternation on Mac's face as he stood with a hand on the pommel, eyeing the stirrup.

"Damn," he cursed again, and Michael stared at him wide-eyed as they both realized he wouldn't be able to mount. Not only would it be unwise to ask his broken ankle to bear the brunt of his weight as he pulled himself into the saddle, but the cast had swelled his foot to a size that couldn't possibly fit the stirrup.

"Why don't we just take your pickup?" she suggested, already stepping away from the little mare.

But Mac would have none of it. "You can't get a feel for the land in a truck."

"But—"

"I've ridden out to check my herd just about every morning of my life, and I'm not about to stop now." She saw his eyes narrow with determination. Using a combination of one crutch and the horse for balance, he hopped around to the other side.

"Easy, boy." He calmed the animal, who'd began to sidestep nervously. He lifted his right foot into the stirrup, turning at an awkward angle.

"Dad, I don't think—" Michael closed his mouth and took the crutch his father handed him.

Mac grabbed the pommel, shifted his weight into the stirrup and, with a mighty heave, swung his casted foot up and over the saddle.

"Thing must weigh twenty pounds," he grumbled, taking the reins. But he returned Michael's proud grin with one of his own.

Nothing was going to stop this man, Sara thought as she mounted with a minimum of fuss. She watched as Michael secured the crutches behind Mac with two thongs of leather, smiling at the way they extended a foot on either side of the gelding's broad rump.

"All set?" Mac asked her.

She nodded and they walked the horses from the stable with its attached corrals across to the barn, passing a tumbledown haystack depleted from winter feeding, a dozen rabbit hutches and a bright green tractor with a flat front tire and a tuft of feathers and sticks on its padded seat. Michael disappeared inside the open doors of the barn and returned a moment later with the injured yearling, tugging the recalcitrant steer toward them by a yellow nylon rope around its neck. He carried a rifle in his free hand.

When he reached them, he slipped the rope from the calf's head and held up the rifle to his father. With casual ease, Mac palmed the gun and shoved it in the worn leather scabbard attached to his saddle by two silver D-rings.

"We'll be back in a couple of hours," he told Michael.

"Right. You want me to check the fence east of Gopher Draw or head over west?"

"West. And be back by noon to spell Jacob at the station."

Michael gave a wave of his hand and ambled to the stable to saddle his horse, his hat pushed down low over his eyes in perfect imitation of his father's. Mac gave his reins a shake and Justice started off at a slow walk, herding the calf before him. Sara's paint mare ambled docilely by his side, following the deep rut that led past the hayfields in back of the house to the wide expanse of open range beyond.

She was silent, enjoying the rhythm of a horse under her, that uniquely jarring motion she hadn't felt in years. The cool morning breeze made her glad of the windbreaker, and she shivered pleasantly.

Soon they left behind the civilized acres of alfalfa combed by straight, evenly spaced creases and crossed onto the blunt, untamed rangeland. The emerald green of the fields gave way to the subtler hues of sage, rabbit brush, scrub oak and twisted cedars. A coarse, gray-green grass covered the rocky ground, undulating in the light breeze, and Justice kept a steady, prodding pressure on the calf to stop it from snacking as they walked. Giving Patches a little nudge with her heels, Sara moved even with the bigger horse.

"What's the rifle for?" she asked. "Rustlers?"

"Rattlers."

Her question had been facetious, but she shifted uneasily in the saddle. "You mean snakes?"

"Uh-huh. Or maybe you need to scare away a coyote that's bothering the calves. Or you let off a shot to signal your location if you run into trouble." He shrugged. "It's handy."

She patted the neck of her horse reassuringly, the emptiness of the land they passed striking her anew. Except for a dust gray rabbit that had darted away with terrified speed, she hadn't seen another living thing. Certainly not a herd of cattle.

Curious, she asked, "How many cattle do you have?"

"About two hundred pairs."

"Pairs?"

"That's a mamma cow and her calf."

"No daddies?"

He grinned at her. "It don't take too many bulls to keep 'em all happy."

She returned his smile. "So, not counting a few busy bulls, you have four hundred head altogether?"

"More or less. Herefords, anyway. I've just started to put together a herd of registered Charolais. I've got thirty-eight head now."

From the way he said it, Sara knew he was proud of those Charolais. She vaguely remembered that Charolais were some special breed of big, white cows. French, she thought. But French or not, four hundred and thirty-eight cows didn't sound like that many to her. Maybe the ranch wasn't as big as she'd thought.

She asked, "So how much land do you own, anyway?"

"Four thousand acres."

"What!" Sara stared at him, then shook her head. "You're kidding me."

"And I lease grazing rights on another thirty-five thousand." He said it casually, as if such astronomical numbers were nothing out of the ordinary.

"No way!" She continued to shake her head, her ponytail swinging from side to side. "That's the entire state of Wyoming!"

Mac laughed. "Not quite. It takes more than a hundred acres of range per cow, you know."

As she continued to regard him skeptically, he said, "Look around." He reached over and lifted the brim of her baseball cap as if it was blocking her view. "It's not exactly Kentucky out here."

She watched the yearling rip off another mouthful of the tough grass. "He seems to like it, anyway. How in heaven's name do you keep track of four hundred little cows in all those acres?"

"Well, it's not like we let 'em go wandering all over the place," he told her. "We've got miles and miles of fence, and we rotate the grazing areas every month so we don't overgraze. This little guy's herd isn't too far from the house this month so he doesn't have much farther to walk."

Sure enough, after another fifteen minutes of following a barbed wire fence due north and chasing the little steer this way and that, Sara spotted the signature rust hides and white faces of Herefords. They stood in scattered clumps, most tearing at the grass and chewing tenaciously, some lying with their legs folded under them in the shade of one of the taller cedars or a scattered clump of boulders. Calves born that spring kept close to their mothers, although occasionally one would break away and leap about, chasing sunbeams.

There was a gate made of rusted pipe just ahead, and Mac leaned over to lift the latch. The gate swung open on its own and they passed through. Mac was careful to push it shut behind them. They walked to within a hundred yards of the first group of cattle before Mac reined Justice to a stop. He slid carefully from the saddle, the patient horse bearing his awkward movements without complaint, and untied the crutches. Their rubber tips sank into the dirt as he approached the calf.

"You're home, boy." He gave him a slap on the rump. A year old, the steer was already weaned and would be sent to market with the rest of the yearlings that fall.

"Hop on down," Mac told her. "I need to stretch for a minute. I can see I'm going to have to rig some kind of a stirrup. The weight of the cast pulling on my leg is starting to hurt like hell."

Sara dismounted and tied her mare to the cedar branch he'd tied Justice to, then joined him as he eased down on a flat boulder. Her thighs were already sore from the friction of her jeans against the saddle, and she could feel muscles tightening in her hips, muscles she hadn't remembered she had. Her sigh was as long as Mac's as she stretched her legs in front of her. The morning was beginning to warm. She took off her windbreaker and tied it around her waist, looking idly after the calf that had run eagerly to join the herd. She could see the jagged oval of shaved hide on its shoulder where the vet had cleaned and doctored its cut. She wished she'd thought to go out and watch the man when he'd checked on the calf yesterday morning.

"Did I ever tell you I wanted to be a vet?" she asked, another long-dormant memory surfacing. "I mean, when I was giving you my life's story the other day?"

"Nope, I don't think so."

"Well, I did. That was my major in college—pre-vet."

"Really? The cat-and-dog type or the horse-and-cow type?"

"Large animal vet," she stated emphatically. "No doubt about it. I was horse crazy as a kid. My parents had a little farm east of Denver and they got me my very own horse when I was twelve. A chestnut mare."

She smiled fondly at the memory. "I'd ride out early in the morning, just like we're doing—it seems like it was always summer back then—and I'd be gone for hours and hours. I'd turn my back on the Rockies and head toward the plains."

She pulled off her cap, dragging the band of her ponytail with it, and ran her fingers through her hair, combing out the tangles. "Those plains went on and on and I never did manage to reach the end of them before I got hungry. I'd come back late for lunch—sunburned, sweaty, smelling like horse." She squinted against the sun, concentrating, trying to bring forth a picture of that girl she could barely remember.

Mac said, "Go on," his voice low as if he didn't want to disturb the flow of words.

She shrugged, unable to focus on more than a few scattered memories, frozen in time like black-and-white photos. "I remember writing in my diary that I was going to be a vet and have a whole stable full of horses, Arabians, if I remember correctly. I was going to have this big old ranch—a real ranch, not a little chicken-and-corn farm like my folks—and I was going to marry a cowboy, a Zane Grey, card-carrying cowboy."

Mac laughed at the way she purposely drawled out her last words. "I thought you said your husband was an English teacher."

"He was." She thought of Greg, with his thinning hair, doelike brown eyes, sharply creased gray suits and a passion for the classics. He was about as far from her story-book hero as she could imagine.

"So how'd that happen? It sounds like you got side-tracked somewhere."

"I married my English Lit professor." She found herself telling him about Greg, a serious, gentle young teaching assistant who'd taught a required English class her first semester in college. "We fell in love and got married at the semester break. I got pregnant almost immediately, so I quit school and..." She frowned. "Well, there was just no time, you know? Laura had asthma when she was little and it was a pretty traumatic period for us, then when she started school, we needed the extra money so I got a part-time secretarial job with the telephone company. Then, well, there were all those bake sales, and PTA meetings, and those horrible faculty teas—"

She let out a puff of air, suddenly impatient with the telling. "To make a long story short, instead of a cowgirl I ended up a professor's wife at one of Denver's oldest and finest institutions eating a lot of little sandwiches with the crusts cut off." She paused and found herself giving a little all-over shake, as if to physically throw off the weight of those stifling, formal teas. She forced a smile. "I did like those sandwiches, though."

Mac wasn't fooled by the smile. He'd heard the strain in her voice as she talked about that time in her life. Just as he'd noticed the dreaminess as she'd described her childhood on horseback. Her speech had lost its cultured edge and her precise diction had slowed and lengthened, ending words with a barely discernible drawl. He could still hear the farm down deep, not completely stifled by those intervening years.

He watched her as she stared into the distance, studying her profile as the wind played with her hair, loose and blowing into tangles. Seeing her against the brilliant blue sky with its motionless clusters of white clouds, he had no trouble imagining her as that young girl galloping across the endless plains. In spite of her patrician looks, it seemed she belonged to the land, just as he did. How had she gotten so far from where she belonged? he wondered. How had she ended up roaming the country in the confines of a truck instead of flying free on that chestnut mare?

His fingers itched to gather her tumbled hair into his fist, to tame it—and her—to stop her restless wandering. He wanted to hold her against him, hold her tight until she stopped struggling and begged to stay right there next to him. He wanted to capture her lips, to feel them open under his and know she'd be there long enough for him to memorize their shape, their texture, their taste.

Instead, he reached for his crutches. "We better head back," he said, his tone more curt than he'd intended. "I've got a pile of chores to do."

Sara nodded and waited for him to mount so she could tie his crutches behind him, then she swung into her saddle with one fluid motion. He found himself admiring the way she rode, with a grace that spoke of more than just hours spent on horseback. She had a natural rapport with horses, and when they returned to the stable and she offered to brush down Justice as well as Patches, he didn't hesitate to turn the big animal over to her. When he checked on the horses after he'd changed the tractor's flat tire, both were gleaming, standing docile and content in their stalls.

"What'd you do to Justice?" Jacob asked while they worked side by side in the corral, early evening lengthening their shadows as they replaced a top rail, gnawed almost through by strong horse teeth. "If a horse could purr, he'd be doin' it."

"Wasn't me, it was Sara," he said around the nail he held in his mouth. "She brushed him down. Patches, too."

He spit out the nail and positioned it against the board, driving it through with three sharp hammer blows.

"Do you think you could ask her to stay a few more days?" Jacob asked.

At Mac's surprised look, he said, "I'm serious. She's awful handy to have around."

The screen door slammed, setting a magpie screeching from its perch on a fence post. Sara's voice floated over to them. "Supper's ready," she called, lengthening the syllables into a song. "Supper time."

"See what I mean?" Jacob grinned at his father, holding his end of the board steady. "Awful handy."

He had to agree when he and Jacob entered the kitchen a few minutes later, tossing their hats brim up on top of the refrigerator. The smell of roast chicken and chili peppers made his mouth water. The table groaned under the weight of softened tortillas, refried beans, tomato salsa and a plate of succulent shredded chicken.

"Wow! Would you look at this!" Michael's voice called to them from the living room. Mac and Jacob exchanged glances, then reluctantly turned their backs on the food and followed the sound of Michael's excited voice.

Mac's eyebrows rose as he surveyed the living room where Michael stood, arms windmilling as he twirled in circles on his heel. "And the upstairs is the same way!" he crowed. "Everything's dusted, vacuumed, spit-and-polished, little vases of flowers all over the place! You should see it. And the bathroom! Dad, that black stuff between the tiles comes off! Did you know that?"

"That's mold, Michael," Sara's dry voice sounded behind them, her light steps moving down the stairs. "All it takes is a squirt or two of bleach."

Mac's tiredness lifted as he watched her walk toward him. He forgot all about his ankle, which had began to throb hours ago. Sara had changed from her jeans into spring green shorts and another one of those blouses with the old-fashioned floral print she seemed to favor, the ones that reminded him of formal English gardens. Her hair was down for the first time, only the sides caught from her face in a gold barrette, and the ends brushed her shoulders with a gentleness his fingers longed to imitate.

Instead, he smiled and said, "The place looks great. But I know you cleaned yesterday. I noticed the shoes were gone from the TV."

"*That* was straightening—*this* was cleaning," she informed him, the difference clear to her. "This afternoon was the first chance I've had to really dig in. It was my penance for leaving the dishes this morning."

"Jeez, Michael, don't touch anything!" Jacob yelled as the younger boy started to sit on the sofa. "You'll mess it up."

"It unmesses," Sara said mildly as Michael hopped up and smoothed the indent in the cushion, but she looked embarrassed by the attention. "Come and eat before it gets cold." She led the way to the kitchen, and Mac wasn't sure if his mouth watered more from the roses drifting after her or the fajitas waiting for him.

He'd have thought Sara would have had enough of cleaning by the time they'd finished the supper dishes and were watching a video in the living room, the boys sprawled on the floor, Mac in his easy chair. But when Jacob and Michael excused themselves to go upstairs for the night, Sara immediately began to straighten up after them. She did it in a distracted way as if her thoughts were not fully on folding the afghan Michael had tossed on the end of the couch or fluffing the pillow Jacob had used. She seemed restless and wandered around the room behind his chair, just out of his line of sight, centering objects, picking up an invisible string from the carpet.

She'd be gone tomorrow, he thought. He doubted if she often stayed in one place this long—she was already antsy and ready to move on. He tested the thought the way a tongue probed a sore tooth, waiting for the stab of pain. Her restlessness was making him edgy, and he folded the newspaper he'd been scanning and let it drop to the floor by his chair.

He couldn't ask her to stay, of course, not when she was so obviously ready to leave. He tried out a few versions in his mind, anyway, though he knew he wouldn't utter any of them. He couldn't. The way his eyes followed her as she moved about the room, drinking her in, absorbing her warmth, her scent, his ear cocked, waiting for her voice—all were danger signs that warned the sooner she left, the better for his peace of mind.

"Can I use your phone?" Sara asked suddenly.

Mac gave a guilty start as if she could somehow read his thoughts. "Sure. Of course." He made a show of rustling up the paper again and flipped to the sports page, reading articles he'd already read. He heard her pick up the phone in the hallway behind him and eavesdropped shamelessly, waiting with her for someone to answer her call.

"Hi, sweetie, it's Mom."

Ah, her daughter. He tried to follow the one-sided conversation.

"No, I never made it that far. I'm staying with a...a friend just outside of Dutch Creek. No one you know. His name— Well, uh, yes, it's a man— No! Of course not. It's not like that at all— Honey, it's a long story. My truck broke down and—

"No, this isn't another example of me going middle-aged crazy." He heard her voice cool perceptibly. "I don't really want— I don't really want to go through this all again, Laura. I've already told you, I *don't know* how long I'll be gone this time—

"Look, I just wanted to see how you were doing." Mac winced at the raw pain in her voice. Couldn't her daughter see how much she was hurting her with her badgering? A protective urge welled inside him. He wanted to grab the phone out of Sara's hand and tell that girl a thing or two. His angry thoughts prevented him from concentrating on the rest of the conversation, which sounded like more of the same, Laura condemning and Sara defending. All he could hear were the tears that sounded closer and closer to the surface.

He heard Sara give his address and phone number then say, "I love you, too, sweetie. I know— I know—" Her tone softened. "I know you do— Take care. I'll call you from Yellowstone when I get there— Well, I'm not sure when, exactly. Soon, though. Bye."

Mac quickly returned his attention to his paper, but he felt her walk past him toward the bookshelf next to the sofa. Her movements were more agitated than before, and her toe tapped the carpet as she scanned the rows of books, running her finger slowly along the spines as if she could absorb their contents. He saw her hand stop at a thick black volume he knew was a layman's book on equine medicine. She pulled it from the shelf and began to leaf through it. Mac saw how quickly she became absorbed, her toe stopping its nervous tap. She moved to the sofa and sat down, her eyes never leaving the book.

"Mac?"

"Hmm?" He tried to sound distracted, as if he weren't vitally aware of her every movement.

"Look at this." She brought the book over and handed it to him, kneeling beside his chair, leaning her elbows on the leather armrest as she studied the diagram with him. "When I was brushing Patches, I noticed she has this same kind of bump on her leg." She pointed with her finger and the movement brought her breasts within a fraction of his arm. "It says it's some kind of calcium deposit."

He studied the picture, trying to concentrate on it instead of her nearness. "I've never noticed, but I'll have the vet check it out the next time he's here."

She nodded and he handed her the book. "Have you ever thought of going back to college and finishing your degree?" he asked, struck by the sudden thought. "Going on to vet school?"

"What?" Sara rocked on her heels and stared at him, startled. "You mean get my license?"

"Sure. You've got the time, you're great with horses—even Jacob noticed it. You'd make a great vet."

She shook her head even while she smiled at his compliment. Goodness, it had been so long since she'd dreamed that dream. She didn't know if it was possible to resurrect the passion she'd once felt. It had been effectively snuffed out by the mounds of starched white shirts to iron and peanut butter and jelly sandwiches to make. She wouldn't know how to begin to breathe life into it again.

"I don't think so." She shut the book and set it on the carpet beside her. "I've just gotten comfortable with all this—the camper and the road and all. It suits me. I don't think I'm ready to try something new." She gave a rueful smile. "I can just hear what Laura would have to say about the idea of me as a coed."

"From what I heard, it sounds as if she's still unhappy with the way things are."

"Laura hasn't been happy with me in a long time. It's always the same thing. Why don't you come home, Mother? How much longer, Mother?"

"And you tell her...." Mac let the question trail off, waiting for her answer.

"I tell her they're going to find my bones in my truck alongside the road somewhere outside of Santa Fe when I'm eighty or so." She said it defiantly, her chin raised, daring him to take Laura's side. But she heard the lack of enthusiasm behind the defiance, as if it was the right answer but no longer the true answer. And that scared her. She might have given up her dream of being a vet, but this dream, this freedom that had tantalized her for so many years during her marriage, she had achieved this dream. Damn it, she had gotten what she wanted, and she wasn't about to give it up.

So when Mac said, "You don't sound very excited about that," Sara lifted her chin higher.

"Maybe it's not all that exciting anymore—but it's a hell of a lot more exciting than a matching washer and dryer and a lawn mower. And maybe it's still more exciting than starting eight years of college. I don't need a career. I've got enough money to live on comfortably for the rest of my life, not extravagantly, but my needs are simple. All I really want— I just want—"

"What?" He asked it as if her answer really mattered to him. He leaned toward her and reached out to cup her chin in his palm, not allowing her gaze to drop from his, forcing her to stare into intense blue eyes that had deepened to midnight. "What?"

"Peace. I just want…peace."

She breathed the words so quietly she wasn't sure she'd spoken them aloud. His thumb brushed across her bottom lip. Her lips parted, opening at his stroke. When his mouth quietly, gently touched hers, she closed her eyes. Peace. When his hands settled onto her shoulders to pull her closer to him, she sighed. Greg's embrace, in spite of her love for him, had often felt like chains. Mac's powerful, roughened hands, hands that held her so tightly she couldn't move, felt like—freedom.

NO RISK, NO OBLIGATION TO BUY...NOW OR EVER!

GUARANTEED

PLAY "ROLL A DOUBLE" AND YOU GET FREE GIFTS! HERE'S HOW TO PLAY:

1. Peel off label from front cover. Place it in space provided at right. With a coin, carefully scratch off the silver dice. Then check the claim chart to see what we have for you – FOUR FREE BOOKS and a mystery gift – ALL YOURS! ALL FREE!

2. Send back this card and you'll receive brand-new Silhouette Romance® novels. These books have a cover price of $3.25 each, but they are yours to keep absolutely free.

3. There's no catch. You're under no obligation to buy anything. We charge nothing – ZERO – for your first shipment. And you don't have to make any minimum number of purchases – not even one!

4. The fact is thousands of readers enjoy receiving books by mail from the Silhouette Reader Service™. They like the convenience of home delivery...they like getting the best new novels BEFORE they're available in stores...and they love our discount prices!

5. We hope that after receiving your free books you'll want to remain a subscriber. But the choice is yours – to continue or cancel, any time at all! So why not take us up on our invitation, with no risk of any kind. You'll be glad you did!

THIS SURPRISE MYSTERY GIFT COULD BE YOURS _FREE_ WHEN YOU PLAY "ROLL A DOUBLE"

"ROLL A DOUBLE!"

Place label here

SCRATCH HERE

SEE CLAIM CHART BELOW

215 CIS CDWG
(U-SIL-R-01/98)

YES! I have placed my label from the front cover into the space provided above and scratched off the silver dice. Please send me all the gifts for which I qualify. I understand that I am under no obligation to purchase any books, as explained on the back and on the opposite page.

NAME

ADDRESS   APT.

CITY   STATE   ZIP

CLAIM CHART

4 FREE BOOKS PLUS MYSTERY BONUS GIFT

3 FREE BOOKS PLUS BONUS GIFT

2 FREE BOOKS   CLAIM NO. 37-829

The Silhouette Reader Service™ — Here's how it works:

Accepting free books places you under no obligation to buy anything. You may keep the books and gift and return the shipping statement marked "cancel." If you do not cancel, about a month later we'll send you 6 additional novels and bill you just $2.67 each plus 25¢ delivery per book and applicable sales tax, if any.* That's the complete price — and compared to cover prices of $3.25 each — quite a bargain! You may cancel at any time, but if you choose to continue, every month we'll send you 6 more books, which you may either purchase at the discount price...or return to us and cancel your subscription.
*Terms and prices subject to change without notice. Sales tax applicable in N.Y.

Chapter Six

"Lordy, Mac, I leave town for a couple days and look what you go and do!"

Sara looked up from where she loaded the breakfast dishes to see the screen door open and a woman walk into the kitchen. The woman was tall and slim, and her straight blond hair hung almost to her waist. Her smiling eyes were a startling, brilliant blue in a suntanned face with perfect Nordic features. In faded jeans, a black cotton work shirt embroidered at the yoke and dangling turquoise and silver earrings, she looked unbearably healthy and vibrantly female.

"Libby!" Mac grinned at his neighbor over the paperwork he had spread out on the kitchen table. "So how was the meeting?"

"Boring as hell. Daddy loved every minute of it." She reached to hold open the door for an old man and woman who were still negotiating the porch stairs. The woman was round-bodied, pink-cheeked, with fuzzy white hair floating around her head and a golden pie clutched between two pot holders. The man was stick-thin but just as pink, and bald as a billiard ball. His pot holders enveloped a casserole dish of lasagna.

"Mornin', Carl. Edith. I hope that's strawberry-rhubarb."

"'Course it is," the old woman huffed, breathing hard as she made her way to the table and sank into a chair. "After forty years, I think I know your favorite."

"You spoil me rotten, Edith. Carl—" Mac raised his voice a notch "—how was Cheyenne?"

The man pulled out a chair, plopped the casserole in the center of the table and reached for the newspaper Mac had pushed aside. "Too damned big and too damned noisy."

"Daddy kept his hearing aid turned off the whole trip," Libby said with an indulgent smile.

"Didn't miss nothing, neither. You goin' to be okay?" he asked Mac with gruff concern.

"Getting by fine," Mac answered.

Carl nodded, dug a pair of reading glasses from the bib pocket of his overalls and opened the paper to the crossword puzzle.

"Can I get anyone a cup of coffee?"

All heads turned in Sara's direction where she still stood at the other end of the kitchen.

"You must be Sara." Libby held out her hand and left the doorway to cross the room and give Sara's hand a firm shake. "I ran into Susie last night. She said she stopped to get gas yesterday and the boys told her you were helping out."

"Sara Shepherd, this is Libby Todd and her parents, Edith and Carl Swanson." Mac made the introductions. "Their place is just down the road."

"Pleased to meet you," Sara said.

"I'm sorry we couldn't get here any sooner. We decided to spend the day in Cheyenne and do some shopping.

Didn't get back until late last night. Saw Susie when I went to get some milk and she told me all about everything. So let's see it." She paused expectantly, making quick little come-here motions with her fingers.

Mac scooted back his chair and stuck out his foot.

Libby bent over the cast, pretending to squint. "Why, it's just a little bitty thing! The way Susie talked, I thought you'd be covered chin-to-toe, with just your eyes peeking out."

"You know Susie likes to make a good story."

She placed her hands on her hips and looked at Mac skeptically. "She said you were a crummy patient. I bet that wasn't a story. Sara, is he behaving himself?"

Sara set three more coffee cups on the table and a full coffeepot on a black trivet. "He works too hard," she said, trying to sound neutral.

"No kidding." Libby picked up the pie from the table and balanced it on top of the lasagna, then carried them both to the refrigerator. She peered inside, stooping to rearrange leftovers to make room for the new pans. "I'm glad you're going to be able to help out for awhile. How long can you stay?" Her voice echoed from inside the refrigerator.

Sara raised her head, startled, as the muffled words reached her. "Uh, not much longer. I—"

Mac spoke at the same time. "She can't. She's got to, uh—"

Sara's gaze flew to his, locked, saw the same consternation she knew must be in her eyes, then skidded away. They avoided looking at each other. So she wasn't the only one who realized they'd been playing with fire last night.

After their kiss—a kiss that had gone on and on, her lips clinging to his, her hands caressing the back of his neck, her body trembling like a high school girl's on a first date—they had pulled away and simply stared at each other. Mac had appeared as stunned by the intensity of that kiss as she was—and as dismayed. If he'd been physically able to get up and make a graceful exit, he would have, she'd known. So she'd done it for him, murmuring good-night and disappearing to her room to stare into the dark until the flowers on the wallpaper lightened from black to gray to dusky pink.

This morning, they'd studiously avoided any mention of that searing intimacy, and she was thankful Libby had stopped by to lighten an atmosphere that had become more strained by the minute.

Libby straightened, pushed the refrigerator door closed with her hip and looked from one to another, her un-plucked eyebrows raised at their stuttering. Sara continued to study the grout pattern on the Mexican tile, noticing that Mac didn't volunteer to elaborate, either.

Finally, Libby spoke, sounding cautious. "Mac, you're going to need some help. If Sara can't stay…''

"Maybe Pa can come help with the chores," her mother volunteered. "Can't you, Pa?"

"Heh?'' Carl Swanson looked up from his paper, peering at his wife over the top of his glasses.

"Help with the chores," she enunciated, her ample bosom resting on the tabletop as she leaned across to shout in her husband's direction.

He cupped a liver-spotted hand around his ear and turned his head toward her. "What's the matter with the horses?''

"Never mind, Daddy." Libby moved to pat her father's shoulder. He licked the end of his pencil and went back to his puzzle.

"I'll be glad to come over in the afternoons," Libby said, but the small frown lines that marred her forehead belied the warm smile on her lips. "And I'll send Rebecca over in the mornings. She'll love that. Did you know my daughter's got a crush on Jacob that won't quit? I heard her talking to— Oh, no, Mac,'' Libby interrupted herself and her frown deepened. ''What about the branding? How are you going to handle it?''

''Yeah, I know.'' Mac sounded sober. ''I've been thinking about that.''

''Everybody's set to help this weekend.'' Libby dropped into a chair and stared at him in concern. ''Remember, next weekend's the dance—you can bet nobody'll be working. Then we've promised to help the Reeds the week after that and do ours the next week. If we put your calves off much longer, they're going to be so big they'll kick the tar out of us!''

''I know, I know. Just slow down, Lib.'' Mac rubbed his jaw, considering, then shook his head. ''It's now or never. All that rain and mud in May put us way behind. It'll have to be this weekend.''

''There's no way you're going to be able to flank those calves in a cast!'' Libby protested.

Sara had helped herself to a cup of coffee, unobtrusively following their conversation. She had vague childhood memories of watching her parents help a neighbor brand once and knew that flanking consisted of jerking a bawling calf off its feet and holding it down while it was branded. If that was Mac's job, there was no way he could do it.

Mac obviously agreed. He said, ''Jacob was after me all last year to let him have a go at it. I guess it's time he gave it a try. I'll do the roping.''

''Twelve hours in the saddle? In a cast? Yeah, right.''

''Dammit, Libby, what else am I supposed to do?''

''Do you ride?''

Sara quickly swallowed a scalding sip of coffee as Libby turned to face her, her blond hair flipping across the back of her chair like a sheet in a brisk breeze.

''Well, I—''

"It would just be through the weekend. If we really bust butt, we should finish up late Sunday night. Is there any way you could rearrange some plans and maybe squeeze out a couple more days here?"

"Libby, stop it. We can't go begging—"

"I can." She ignored Mac and waited for Sara's answer.

"I don't have any fixed schedule, exactly." Sara ran her stinging tongue along the back of her teeth. "But I've never had anything to do with branding before. I don't know if I'd be much help."

"We just need another pair of hands," Libby assured her. "You could give the vaccinations. Just a quick in-out jab. Or bring over the hot irons. Don't worry, we'll find something you're good at."

Sara hesitated. Libby seemed so brash and unassuming, and there was no doubt Mac needed help. But last night had shown her how dangerous her little walk on the wild side could be. She'd been convinced a healthy attraction between them could be contained—at their age they weren't exactly at the mercy of their hormones—but now she wasn't so sure. She'd been aware of him all morning, her eyes unable to keep from straying to his mouth again and again. At the sight of its firm fullness, places began to tingle she'd forgotten were supposed to tingle.

Mac chose that moment to meet her eyes. His chin was tilted at a stubborn angle, his lips clamped shut like a child refusing to take his medicine. He refused to ask her to stay. He refused to admit he needed help. And Sara felt herself melt in the face of such adamant, pigheaded, stubborn male pride. What a cowboy! Zane would be proud of him.

It looked like it was up to her and Libby to ensure his pride didn't get in the way of common sense. For heaven's sake, they had two teenage boys for chaperons and enough work to make sure they both dropped into bed exhausted at night with nothing on their minds but sleep. It had only been a kiss, and she knew she was in no danger of it ever turning into anything more. Mac, taken alone, might be a potent attraction, but he came attached with a ranch house that made caring for her little brick house by the university look like a walk in the park. No, there was nothing here she couldn't easily turn her back on when the time came.

"I'd be glad to stay for the branding," she said. "A few more days, one way or the other, won't make any difference to my plans."

"Great!" Libby slapped her palms on her thighs.

Mac didn't smile. His eyes were still on her face. "Thanks," he said. "Appreciate it." But the heat in his look was much warmer than appreciation, and her response, a delicious curling in the pit of her stomach, was more than a friend helping a friend. She hoped she hadn't just made a big mistake.

"Guess we better be getting back," Libby said, pushing aside her coffee cup and rising. "If I let Rebecca out of my sight for more than a minute, she's either dyeing something, tattooing something or piercing another body part. No, don't get up," she told Mac as he made a move for his crutches, "we know our way to the door."

While she waited for her parents, Libby reached across Mac to pick up a pen that rested on his stack of papers. "Don't tell me I'm the first," she said, bending down to peer at his cast. "I expected the boys to have scribbled all over it by now." With a flourish, she scrawled her name across the bumpy plaster, then handed the pen to Sara.

"See you Friday," Libby told her. "It'll be fun. Nothing like spending a weekend wrestling a couple hundred calves."

After goodbyes were said and the screen door slammed for the last time, Sara stood beside the table, pen in hand, blinking slightly from the force of Libby's personality.

Mac still had his leg stretched in front of him, Libby's signature big and bold across the dirt-smudged cast.

"Your turn?" he asked, lifting his foot to rest on the chair beside him.

She didn't know why she felt herself blushing as she knelt next to him and hesitantly added her name, writing careful, tidy letters with the self-consciousness of a child at the blackboard in front of the class. Next to Libby's scrawl, her name looked cramped and fussy.

"Hmm." Mac peered at both sides of the cast. "It still looks a little bare, don't you think?"

With a small smile, she drew a cartoonish truck with an oversize camper next to her name. Then she sketched a limp boot caught under the front tire, its pointed toe elongated to form an elephant's snout.

"All right, that's enough," Mac protested with a laugh. "I'm still in mourning over that boot."

She looked up and smiled into his eyes, but her smile froze as she realized how intimately close their position was, how similar to last night, and how much she yearned for him to lean forward again and claim her lips as he had then. She snapped upright and took a quick step away from Mac.

For a moment, Mac thought the small groan he heard was from his own throat as Sara flinched away from him. But he saw the way her hands reached behind her to massage her hips and round bottom as stiff muscles must have protested her movements.

"Sorry," she grimaced. "Yesterday was the first time I've been in a saddle in— Well, in a long, long time." She gathered the empty coffee cups from the table and took them to the dishwasher.

Mac watched as she continued to idly rub the back of her khaki shorts with one hand while she set the cups in the rack then began to wipe at the stove top with a dishrag.

His eyes followed the motion of her pink-tipped fingers over her shorts, and he found his fingers clenching into fists to stop their unconscious imitation of her movements as he imagined his hand cupping and squeezing and—

This time he did groan. Lord, the rest of the week with her in his house! He didn't know how he was going to spend another night knowing she slept just down the hallway from him. The only thing that had gotten him through last night was concentrating on the fact that she would be gone today and he wouldn't have to do it again.

That kiss had been a potent warning to them both that she should leave, run for the hills, hightail it out of the entire state of Wyoming, for that matter. He should have tried harder to stop Libby, but the woman was like a steamroller. She'd put Sara in a position where it was impossible to say no. He tried to dredge up some irritation at Libby's strong-arm tactics, but Sara's every movement sidetracked him.

He watched the muscles in her bare arm as she dragged the wet cloth over the stove, her fingers dipping into grooves around the burners, circling the knobs— Stop it! he ordered himself. There was nothing erotic about cleaning a stove! If it wasn't for his cast, he thought in disgust, he'd probably be chasing her around the kitchen like some manor dandy after the downstairs maid.

"That's enough," he growled. "The damn thing sparkles so much now it hurts my eyes. You're more than earning your bathtub rights."

Sara didn't turn around. "I can't help myself." She said it lightly, but there was a sober undertone as she rinsed the rag and proceeded to wipe the already clean counter.

"Can't help yourself?" He frowned. "You make cleaning sound like an obsession."

She shrugged. "Obsession, obsessive-compulsive disorder, perfectionism—there are a lot of different names."

He stared at her, confused. "You're serious, aren't you?"

"Afraid so." She gave him an apologetic smile over her shoulder. "Everything's got to be just right—just so—before I can relax."

His frown deepened, and he pressed, trying to understand. "You mean it's got to be clean? Straightened up?"

"Not just clean. It's more than that." She pushed her bangs off her forehead with an impatient hand and dropped the rag into the sink. "It's got to be..." She hesitated and Mac knew she didn't even notice the way she picked the rag up again and began to carefully fold it and drape it neatly over the faucet. "It's got to be *right*."

"Right?"

"Right." She turned her back to the sink and leaned against it. "I remember when I was a child and my mother would hand me a sandwich for lunch. First thing I'd do is open that sandwich up and start to rebuild it."

She smiled wryly at the memory. "The circle of bologna would have to be exactly centered on the bread—white bread not wheat—the mayonnaise spread evenly from side to side, the lettuce completely covering the bologna, and the top slice had to fit as perfectly as one of those hand-carved lacquer boxes. And oh, the tears if something should start to slip or drip. I'd have to start all over again." Her shrug was matter-of-fact. "It had to be...right."

Mac thought of Michael and Jacob as babies, eating spaghetti with their fingers, a spoon clutched forgotten in the other chubby little hand, or now, grabbing a piece of bologna straight from the plastic package and wrapping it around a hunk of cheese on the way out the door. That's the way all children he knew acted. "So you were like this even as a little kid?"

"My mother swears I was born this way. She tells me it would take fifteen minutes to get my shoes on in the morning when I was a toddler. She said the seam at the end of my sock had to go exactly on top of my toes or I'd scream bloody murder. She'd have to take it off over and over again until it was just right—'' Sara gave a rueful laugh. "I made her crazy."

He scratched his chin, having trouble imagining such a scene. "But there has to be some reason, doesn't there? There was no—"

Sara shook her head, not waiting for him to finish his question. "No dysfunctional childhood, no trauma in the womb, no bad relationship with a parent, no domineering relative." Her voice had taken on a singsong quality as she reeled off the psycho-babble list. "Greg used to ask me things like that for hours, trying to find some dark secret in my past. But it makes me really impatient to play the victim, to try to blame this on somebody else. As far back as I can remember I've liked things black-and-white, right and wrong, yes and no. It's just the way I am. It doesn't really bother me a bit. It doesn't cramp my life-style at all."

"Not when your life-style is living out of a suitcase," he agreed.

"I don't live out of a suitcase."

But he stared at her, thunderstruck, as he realized the significance of his offhand remark. He got it now. He'd discovered the reason for her odd travels, the rootlessness that had nagged at him ever since they met.

"That's it, isn't it!" He gave the table a thump of triumph. "That's what this is all about."

"What are you talking about?" Sara frowned.

"That's why you sold everything, why you took off. Instead of trying to relax your standards, you decided to narrow your world down so you only have a few things to make right. Instead of getting rid of the obsession, you got rid of the things you obsessed about." He began to tick off on his fingers, "No house, no possessions, no messy relationships, no—"

"Well, thank you, Dr. Wallace, for that brilliant analysis," Sara interrupted, her voice scathing.

Her huffy tone had him quickly backpeddling, and he reined in his excitement. "Hey, I didn't mean it like that, but don't you see—"

"I don't need you to take up where Greg left off."

"I only meant—"

"I'm very well aware of why I do what I do. When you only have three pairs of shoes, it doesn't take long to get them in a straight line." She smiled at him with mock sweetness. "And now that we've psychoanalyzed my behavior and established that I'm a total wacko, let's talk about you."

"Me?" He laughed, but he felt a twinge of unease at the look in Sara's eyes. "I'm perfectly normal. Great kids, great ranch, great life..."

"Oh, really?" Sara gave an unladylike snort. "Let's see, then, how about—Ronda?"

He jerked so hard, his cast, which was still propped on the chair, slipped and fell to the floor. "Damn! Ow! Damn!"

Sara merely looked at him with raised eyebrows, but he could tell she relished her revenge.

"Now that's what I call a knee-jerk reaction," she said. "What's the matter? Did I touch a sore spot? A little trouble in paradise?"

"All right, all right, I see your point." He wanted out of this conversation—right now. "Nobody likes to be put under the microscope. So I'll just go ahead and admit it—maybe I haven't dealt with the divorce very well. There. We've saved thousands in therapy and didn't need a twelve-step program to do it."

But Sara didn't seem ready to let it go that easy. "Very

well? For goodness' sake, Mac, you've been divorced for five years. Eligible bachelors must be scarce as hens' teeth out here. You must have women swarming all over you, but you're still single and just the name of your ex-wife still gets a rise out of you." She pretended to look at him over the top of a pair of glasses. "There's obviously some residual anger here we need to deal with."

He could hear the influence of her late husband in her clinical tone and was reminded of how much he disliked the man even though he'd never met him.

"It's not residual anything. It's hard to get dumped, that's all." He forced a smile. "Sounds like a country western song, doesn't it?"

"Lots of wives leave their husbands, Mac, and the husbands get over it." Sara moved to the table and pulled out a chair. She leaned her elbows on the top and studied him. "What gives?"

"Nothing gives. It's just a sore spot. It's hard for a man to admit he can't keep his woman." There, he'd said it. Now maybe she'd let him alone. But no, he could tell by the look in those gray eyes that had tempered to steel—she'd just gotten started on him.

"Keep his woman?"

"I know that sounds old-fashioned—"

"Chauvinistic."

"Okay, chauvinistic. But there it is. She left me."

"Not you. You said Ronda left because she got tired of the ranch, the isolation—"

Mac felt his lip curl. "That's what she said." Then he cursed himself silently when he saw the way Sara sat up straighter, as alert as a hound on the scent.

"So it was more than that?" she asked. "Because I can sort of understand her point. It's a hard life, even if she was raised on a ranch."

He almost laughed. He'd understood Ronda's decision

only too well. In fact, he hadn't really blamed her. The work, the winters, the solitude—hell, he'd understood how a woman could have enough of that. He'd believed her when she'd listed all the reasons she had to go. But she'd never listed the real reason—him. What she'd really wanted to leave was him. What she'd had enough of was him. Just him.

"And, as I said before," Sara went on, "it happens all the time—to a lot of men."

"Not to me," he snapped.

"Not to you?" Sara's voice was sharp. "So this is all about a bruised ego? You do sound like one of those poor-me country western songs."

He reached under the table for his crutches. "Let it go, Sara," he said, feeling suddenly bone weary. His ankle ached as he pulled himself to his feet. "It was a long time ago."

Sara slipped into the ranch's rhythm without conscious effort, cooking, cleaning, helping at the station, and best of all, riding every day. Sometimes she went out with one of the boys to check the herd or take salt to the cattle, but sometimes she just rode. Galloping across the dips and swells of empty rangeland, she was surprised to discover the same peace she found so gratifying and intoxicating in her travels.

It was disconcerting to find such freedom someplace besides the open road. Sometimes she caught herself wondering if it was possible to run while staying in one place. If maybe it was possible to take a deep breath while surrounded by ranch house walls. If it was possible to care for someone without drowning in his demands.

Mac's overwhelming presence did nothing to help her sort out her jumbled thoughts. He met her as she came back from a ride one afternoon, striding out of the barn in time to grab the reins of her sweating mare, holding the prancing horse still while she prepared to dismount.

"Thanks," she said.

"Good ride?"

"Wonderful." She slid out of the saddle and turned, only to find him standing so close she took a quick step back.

Her boot heel twisted and she stumbled. As Mac reached out to steady her, his crutch slid from under his arm and slapped against the side of the already excited mare. Jerking her head in fright, Patches yanked the reins from his other hand. Off balance, Mac swayed, his eyes as wide as the mare's, and landed with an audible thud as the backside of his jeans connected with the hard dirt.

"Oh, my, are you all right?" She knelt on the ground beside him, trying to suppress a grin when she saw it was only his dignity that had been injured. She reached out a hand. "Mac, you've got to stop trying to help me before you kill yourself."

"You're right. Every time I do, I end up on my butt." He grinned back. "You're a dangerous woman, Sara Shepherd."

But as their gazes met and locked, her smile faltered. His blue eyes darkened, deepened, and she felt her heart leap in response. The moment hung, suspended between them, focusing the entire ranch into no more than the space that separated her body from his.

"Damned dangerous," he breathed. He took her offered hand and pulled her to him, and his lips covered hers.

Her breathing was still fast from the exertion of the ride, but she couldn't seem to get enough air. Her heart pounded in her chest as he turned her across his lap, his arm cradling her head, his tongue seducing hers. She never gave a thought to shutting her lips to him. Instead, she raised her arms and pulled his head closer, dimly aware that she'd pushed his hat from his head to weave her fingers through his hair.

The feel of his mouth on hers, his tongue against hers, was like an extension of the ride she'd just finished, elemental and earthy. His hips and thighs beneath her moved in the same sensuous, primitive rhythm.

With a groan, he pushed her down and shifted over her, and the hard-packed dirt under her seemed right. The strength and weight of him on top of her seemed right. The smell of horse and sweat and dust seemed right. She wanted raw, powerful, primal sensation. She wanted the hot sun to caress her bare skin, the dirt to grind its way into the pores of her back, the grit to work into her hair. When Mac started to unbutton her shirt and pull it aside, exposing her to his sight, as burning as the sun could ever be, it seemed right.

She wanted him to move with her, to feel his muscles bunch and flex against hers like the horse between her legs only moments before. She wanted to wrap her legs around his just as tightly and hold on while he took her to new places and showed her new sensations. Could she run while staying in one place? she'd wondered. Now she knew she could fly—as long as Mac held her in his arms.

"Stop that," Mac growled, and she opened her eyes in confusion as a blast of hot, horsey breath bathed her face. "Go on, girl, git out of here." Mac levered himself up on one arm and pushed aside the curious mare, who'd come to nuzzle the back of his neck, standing over them where they lay, the dropped reins trailing in the dirt.

With a reluctant-sounding groan, Mac rolled off her and sat up. Sara squinted in the sun, now full on her face without the bulk of his shadow to block it. She struggled to sit up, sanity returning with the glare, and she quickly buttoned her blouse and tucked it into her jeans.

Mac picked up his hat from the ground and swatted again at Patches. "Git!"

The horse took two purposeful steps backward, then stopped, refusing to budge, glaring at Mac with reproachful eyes.

Sara laughed shakily. "She's jealous." Scrambling to her feet, she picked up his crutches and once again held out a hand.

Mac dusted his hat against his jeans and settled it on his head before he took her offered hand, letting her help him to his feet.

For a moment she swayed forward as his weight pulled against her arm. His eyes met hers. She planted her feet more firmly and he eased up to a stand.

"That's right, Sara," he said quietly, "don't be dropping me. I bruise easy."

Friday dawned sparkling and cloudless, promising a hot day to come. By seven o'clock, the house had filled with people. Libby and her family had been the first to arrive. She'd gone out to the barn with her father to help Mac load the truck with supplies. Her daughter, Rebecca, a girl with an angelic face, a shocking blue streak down the part of her blond hair and a row of earrings in one ear, followed Jacob around with unconcealed adoration. Libby's mother commandeered the kitchen, pulling out the huge pans Sara had noticed in the pantry and assumed were for bathing the dogs, and began to braise enormous slabs of meat. By the time the Reeds arrived, a whip-thin man with a bushy black mustache and a taciturn son with a few dark wisps on his upper lip, they were ready to ride out en masse.

The rest of the day passed in hot, sweaty, foul-smelling confusion. Libby and Mac, who'd welded up a contraption on his stirrup for his cast, took turns roping the recalcitrant calves and dragging them over for Jacob or the Reed boy to flank. Michael would grab a handful of skin from the calf's rib and jab it with a needle, vaccinating it for black-leg. Sara had been assigned the job of carrying the hot irons back and forth from the barrel, where they were heated with a propane burner, to old Carl Swanson.

Libby's father, bald head protected from the sun by a disreputable-looking straw hat, would take the red-hot iron from her and hold it to the calf's side, the unique stench of singed hair billowing up to choke them all. His knife would flash in his gnarled hand, efficiently castrating the calf, then, with two, quick downward strokes, he would remove the horn nubs. The stunned calf, barely realizing it was free after Jacob removed his knee from its neck, would stand and shake its head, splattering them all with drops of blood whenever the horning knife cut a little deep.

The dust, churned up by the combined feet of cattle, horses and humans, was thick with manure and urine. By noon, when Edith drove up with a truck loaded with beef stew, buttered bread, apple pie and coolers full of iced tea, Sara's eyes were red and watering and her sinuses were packed.

Saturday and Sunday passed in the same exhausting blur. It was late Sunday night when they finally had the last horse unsaddled, supplies stored, branding irons hung on their hooks in the barn and the last massive cooking pot on its shelf in the pantry. They were gathered in the kitchen, the adults slumped in chairs with their legs stretched out, ice-cold beers in their hands, Mac's cast a filthy gray that obliterated all signatures. The youngsters sat cross-legged on the floor, powdered from head to toe with dust so thick Rebecca's blue stripe faded into insignificance.

"I'm glad we get a break next weekend," Libby said, holding the chilled can against her forehead. "I'm looking forward to the dance."

"Me, too," Rebecca said with a sideways look at Jacob.

"I'm anticipatin' that punch Susie always makes up," Libby's father added with a cackle. "Heard tell she orders the alcohol from one of those medical supply catalogs she gets at the hospital. And while I'm on the subject, Mac, you got anything a mite stronger to cut through this cow pie I got lodged in my lungs?"

"Carl, you know what the doctor said about drinking," his wife cautioned.

"Hell, old woman, a shot of good whiskey's medicinal, and I've got me some refills left on my prescription."

"Jacob," Mac said, "there's a bottle in the cupboard over the refrigerator. Fetch it for Carl, please."

Jacob obediently got to his feet, took the bottle and glasses and brought them over to the table where the men sat. Dust tracked across the floor with every step and he left a smudged fingerprint on every cupboard door he touched. Before he flopped down, he pulled his gloves from the back pocket of his jeans and tossed them down beside him. As he pried off his boots, a stream of fine sand and small pebbles cascaded from them.

"Watch it, Jacob," Mac said with a frown, "you're trashing the kitchen." He glanced at Sara where she sat on the countertop next to the stove. "Sorry, Sara."

She smiled at him, or at least she tried to smile. Her muscles ached so much she wasn't sure if the corners of her mouth moved upward or not. "It doesn't matter," she said. "We'll catch it later."

Mac's eyes widened and his hand stopped its movement to bring the can of beer to his lips. "Really?"

She shrugged. She was too tired to be a perfectionist tonight. All she wanted was a shower and bed, in that order, and she didn't give a damn if the entire state of Wyoming got tracked into the kitchen.

"Ah, that aroma! Is it eau de burned hair I smell wafting

over this convivial gathering?'' A bulbous nose pressed itself against the open screen door, knocking a tweed driving cap askew.

"Cyrus! It's Cyrus!" Michael jumped to his feet and ran to fling the door open. "What are you doing here? It's not August!"

"I heard the call of the wild, my boy, and I couldn't resist. Hello, hello, everyone." Cyrus Bennington stepped through the door, his long, thin face wreathed in smiles. He wore laced, rubber-soled boots, brown corduroy pants and a tweed jacket with leather patches at the elbows. The well-chewed end of a pipe stuck from the breast pocket of the jacket. The professor swept his cap from his thinning gray hair and greeted the tired group with his trademark effusiveness.

When he spied Sara perched on the counter, his faded green eyes twinkled even more. "Sara, my pet! Do forgive me if I don't give you a hug in your present native state, but I am so very pleased to see you're still here." He pressed a cheek tentatively against hers. "But I am surprised, *in extremus*. Don't tell me Mac and his family have managed to curb your wanderlust?"

"Only momentarily." She smiled at the colorful man who'd been such an odd contrast to her husband and such a dear friend. "Truly, your timing is perfect, though. The guest room is all yours. I'll be leaving first thing in the morning."

Chapter Seven

"No way, Sara!" Michael wailed. "I can't go back to eating tuna. I just can't!"

"Please, Sara," Jacob added. "Dad's still a cripple. You can't leave us alone yet."

"I'm not a cripple!"

"Darn near. Sara, we *need* you."

Everything in Mac wanted to add his cry to his sons'. They did need her. He needed her. His eyes fastened on Sara, long legs dangling above the floor. Her hair stuck at odd angles from her short braid, and her bangs lay flat against her forehead, plastered from the combination of her hat and a day's worth of sweat. Her nose and cheeks were sunburned and dust emphasized the fine lines around her eyes and mouth. Her jeans were caked with grime, dried blood and grass stains, and her shirt had a slash across one sleeve where a hot iron had singed the material.

She looked so weary, so lovely, so much a part of his life, he felt his mouth go dry with want. He thought of the way she'd worked for the last three days, dawn to past dark, alongside his family and his neighbors, unflagging, without complaint. He thought of the way she'd worked all week, making his home run smoother than he'd ever remembered, greeting him as he came through the door at night with a smile and a hot meal. He thought of the way she'd galloped into the yard that day, both her and the horse breathing hard and radiating pure joy, bringing a smile to his face just to look at her— God, how very much he needed her.

And how had it happened? He'd tried to keep his guard firmly in place, but she kept slipping through. Like that evening when he'd been unable to resist kissing her as she'd kneeled beside his chair, the scent of warm roses clinging to her hair, her lips so full, so close, so petal soft— And then the afternoon outside the barn— Sweet Lord, that memory still tormented him, asleep or awake. Somehow, he found himself wanting a woman who didn't want to stay any more than Ronda had. Was this his own personal hell? Some kind of curse?

Sara had made it clear from the beginning that she was on a journey—and that, while she might make an occasional detour, she was nowhere near the end of it. He'd told himself over and over again that a woman on the run from her past and herself was the last person he could let himself or his sons need. Hadn't he been listening?

His gaze caught hers, but he wasn't sure if she saw his turmoil, the desire he fought so hard his teeth clenched with the effort, the unwise longing for just a few more days. He forced himself to look away, to pay attention to the conversation.

"You really ought to stay until the dance on Friday," Libby said as she sprawled in a chair at the table. "All the tourists come down from Yellowstone. It's the biggest thing to happen round these parts all summer."

"That's true, Sara," Cyrus assured her. "The Dutch

Creek Midsummer's Festival is quite a to-do. In fact, it's the reason I made the trek up here.''

"You're going to the dance, Uncle Cyrus?" Jacob asked the professor, surprise in his voice.

"Indeed." Cyrus did a quick shuffle with an imaginary partner, the rubber soles of his boots squeaking against the tile floor. "I cut a mean rug, if I do say so myself."

But Sara still shook her head. "It's time to go. Besides, I've got your room," she told the man. "Mac said you always stay with them when you visit."

Mac thought Cyrus looked flustered as he took his pipe from the pocket of his jacket and clamped it between his teeth. "Well, actually—" he sucked deeply on the cold pipe "—actually, I won't be in need of Mac's hospitality on this trip."

"Where are you staying, then?" Jacob asked as they all stared at him.

Cyrus took the pipe from his mouth and fiddled with it, turning the bowl in his hand while his cheeks reddened, making his long sideburns appear even whiter and fluffier. "I've received an invitation to accompany Miss Monroe to the dance, and it seems she has a guest room she's graciously made available to me for the week."

"You're staying with Susie?" Mac tried to imagine Susie, as short and wide as Cyrus was thin and tall, her sensible white nurse's shoes coyly slipping between Cyrus's Wellingtons, gliding around the floor of the high school gym in the professor's arms. It was a difficult picture. "So how'd this happen?"

"I made Suzanne's acquaintance last August when Michael's chicken enchiladas required that rather hasty trip to the emergency room."

"That's right," Mac nodded, "I remember. She pumped your stomach."

"Quite." Cyrus had regained his equilibrium and joined

the tired and dirty group at the kitchen table, hitching his corduroys at the knees as he lowered himself into a straight-back chair. He went on, "That unfortunate culinary experience led to our correspondence, and it seems a long-distance *affaire de couer* has flourished. So, you see, Sara love, there's no need for you to leave on my account. You should stay and enjoy the dance."

"And you know what, Sara?" Libby jumped in with a spark of her customary enthusiasm. "We could really use some help with the decorations. Isn't that right, Mom?" She didn't wait for her mother's reply. "I got dragged onto the decorating committee and we have all these table skirts to sew. Red checks. Makes your eyes cross after awhile. At this rate, we're barely going to finish them in time. If you had just a couple extra days—"

"I was sort of hoping you could help me brush up on my dancing, too," Jacob added, glancing at Libby's daughter out of the corner of his eye. "And Michael could use a few pointers. He does this weird sort of waddle, looks like a pregnant duck."

"I don't, either," the younger boy protested, throwing a glove at his brother as the adults laughed. "I—"

"That's enough," Mac interrupted. He'd been watching Sara and saw the look of panic cloud her eyes as his friends and family clamored for her help. They didn't realize, couldn't know, how overwhelming their demands were for someone who could never be satisfied with anything less than perfection. He bet she was aching for the pristine, familiar safety of her camper right now. He needed to ignore his own ache, the one that had lodged permanently in his gut and lower. He had to let her go.

"I want you all to stop this right now," he ordered. "Listen to yourselves. Asking Sara to stay so she can cook and clean for us, and sew, and teach the fandango— What does she get in return?"

Michael looked at his father, his eyes wide, and spread his arms to encompass them all. "She gets us," he said matter-of-factly, as if the answer should be obvious.

Sara joined the others as they laughed at the boy's innocence.

"Lucky her." Jacob threw the glove at his younger brother.

But Sara looked at the smiling faces surrounding her and thought, indeed, the friendship of the odd assortment gathered in Mac's kitchen was ample repayment for her labor. And if she had come to care about them all in just these few short days, what would happen if she were to stay longer? She felt Mac watching her, but refused to meet his eyes. The dark hunger she'd seen in them a moment ago had sent waves of erotic sensation to the very tips of her scuffed boots. Another week buffeted by those waves, longing to let them wash over her until she drowned in the feeling—it was more than she could endure.

"I've enjoyed helping out," she said, "but I—I need to go." Now she did seek out Mac—surely he understood. But his face was inscrutable, his midnight blue eyes almost black, as remote and distant as the night sky.

"Well, if you change your mind, let me know." Libby pushed herself to her feet. "Let's go, folks, I'm ready for bed."

Chairs scraped as Libby's family said their goodbyes and made their way out the door. Their truck growled to life, gravel spurted under wide tires, dust hung low in the warm air, and the kitchen seemed suddenly quiet. Sara stood next to Mac and the boys by the screen door, one hand lifted in a last wave, the other hand on Michael's shoulder. With the warm, solid presence of Mac at her back, she felt much too much like she belonged.

"How about if you stay as our guest?" Michael's voice

was soft and hesitant. He tilted his head to look at her, his freckles smudged with dirt on his sunburned, earnest face. "I mean, you don't have to do any of the chores or anything. It's..." He seemed to struggle with the words. "It's nice having you around, all the flowers and stuff—"

"Sara has her own plans for the summer." Mac cut him off, but his voice was gentle. "Come on, boys." He swung around on his crutches. "I'll go upstairs with you and make sure you cut through at least one of those layers of dirt before bed. Cyrus, make yourself at home. I'll be back in a minute."

She watched them leave, father and sons, so much alike, a family— Suddenly, she didn't feel like she belonged at all. Her movements brisk, she began to gather up the iced tea glasses with their melting cubes and smudged fingerprints and carry them to the sink. Cyrus stood to help her, tossing empty beer cans into the recycling bin.

"Why the big hurry to hit the dusty trail, Sara?" he asked, letting the cans fall with a clatter.

"I'm not in a hurry. I've been here over a week as it is."

"That's not so long. It certainly sounds as if you've been earning your keep." She ignored the speculative glance he sent her way, but she couldn't ignore his next words. "You know, maybe you should take a little more time. Give them a chance."

"A chance?" She turned from the sink and stared at him in surprise. "A chance to do what?"

"To grow on you."

"For God's sake, Cyrus." Her words tumbled out before she could stop them. "That's why I have to go."

"Ah." Cyrus nodded, sounding wise and scholarly and irritatingly smug.

"Stop that." Suddenly too tired to stand, she left the glasses in the sink, left the ice cubes to melt into a yellow-brown pool and lowered herself into a chair at the table. "The last thing I need is to get any closer to this family when I'll have to leave sooner or later," she said wearily. "I've been all set to go a dozen times already, then somebody talks me into staying. It's getting farcical. Leave, stay, leave, stay." She slumped forward, propping her elbows on the table and rubbing her temples. "Mac must think he's never going to get rid of me."

Cyrus sat across from her, regarding her with kind yet determined calm. "I don't think Mac's in any hurry to have you go."

"You heard him. He said I had my own plans. He agreed with me. *He* didn't ask me to stay." She ignored the sting she felt at that.

"Not with words, maybe." Cyrus shrugged.

She felt her cheeks warm at the thought that anyone had intercepted the look Mac had given her. She reached for the salt shaker in the middle of the table and began to run it around the wet rings left by the glasses.

Cyrus reached for her hand, stopping her nervous movements. "Are you really going to hide inside that sardine can the rest of your life? Is that what you want, Sara? Really?"

Her head snapped up and she glared at him. "I'll tell you what I *don't* want." She encompassed the filthy kitchen with a sweep of her hand. "I don't want this again."

"Don't want what? A family?" he asked gently. "Love?"

She felt her throat tighten, but swallowed and forced the words out, her voice thin. "Too much goes with it."

"Maybe it wouldn't be too much this time."

"Why wouldn't it?" Her laugh sounded hard even to her own ears. "What would be different? Give me a month or two and I'd be putting shelf liner under the haystack and plastic seat covers on the tractor. I haven't changed."

"Maybe you haven't, but things have."

"What things? I—"

Cyrus held up his hand to stop her protest. "Mac isn't Greg, you know."

"That's for sure."

"And the boys aren't Laura. And this ranch is a world away from the university. You can't tell how you'll react."

"I know myself," she said firmly, trying to block out his words.

"But you don't know them. Not really. Listen to me, Sara." She'd never seen Cyrus so earnest, and she pulled her hand away from his, trying to distance herself physically and mentally from his uncomfortable intensity. He went on, "Greg was my best friend but he treated you abominably."

"Cyrus—"

"Abominably. In all the ways that mattered. You weren't exactly a free spirit when you got married, but Greg brought out the very worst in you." Cyrus snorted. "Those ridiculous starched shirts of his, color-coordinated ties, everything just so— That came from him, not you! You went straight from trying to please him as your teacher to trying to please him as your husband. And he deliberately encouraged the very traits that ended up your undoing until you saw no way out but to run. And Laura—"

"She was sick!" Sara jumped to the defense of her daughter.

"She's not sick now," he said pointedly, "and she still gives you no support. It's time to think about yourself."

Sara smiled at his unintentional irony. "That's what Laura says I'm doing."

"Ha! Hiding is what you're doing. For two years now.

I don't think you have any idea how you'd react to a normal life again. Stay for the week, Sara. For yourself. Think of it as a test."

"What's a test?"

She jumped as Mac's voice sounded behind her.

"I think Sara should spend a few more days here to see if she's ready to join the real world again."

"My world's just as real as yours, Cyrus."

Cyrus ignored her, speaking to Mac over her head as if she wasn't in the room. "She's hardly spent longer than overnight in one place in years, you know. It's time to see what's what."

"Playing house for another week at Mac's won't tell me anything," she protested. "It's not the same. And besides, gentlemen, this is it, this is me, phobias and all. I don't *want* to change." Damn, but Cyrus could take his professorial attitude just a bit too far. She wasn't one of his students, running to him to be molded and guided through life. "I *like* my phobias. I don't want to get comfortable with mess and clutter and mismatched socks. I like me just fine this way."

"We like you, too," Cyrus agreed promptly. "That's why we'd like you to have a permanent address again, so we can see more of you. Now, you owe it to yourself to give this a try. Mac will help you, won't you, Mac?"

Mac still stood behind her. She couldn't see his eyes, but his voice was quiet as he said, "I'll do whatever Sara wants."

"Ha! See?" Cyrus exclaimed. "I told you he was nothing like Greg. When did you ever hear Greg say something like that?"

"This is silly." She jumped up, too agitated to sit still. What was the matter with Cyrus, putting her in this awkward position? She turned to Mac, grounding herself against the electricity she felt whenever she looked at him.

"First I stay to help you, and now I'm supposed to stay so you can help me? Enough's enough. I don't need help—I need to leave." *While I still can*, she added silently, but she had a sinking feeling she was protesting too much. And both men knew it.

Cyrus stood and brushed at invisible wrinkles on his pants. "You always were too stubborn for your own good, but I have faith in Mac's persuasive powers. Now, I must go. Suzanne's waiting for me with a hot cup of tea." He took her gingerly by the shoulders and kissed the air near her grimy cheek, then shook Mac's even grimier hand. "I trust I'll see you both at the dance Friday, if not before."

As Cyrus left, Mac saw him remove a snowy-white handkerchief from the pocket of his jacket and carefully wipe his hands. Mac's amused smile faded at the sound of Sara's sigh. He glanced at her sharply. She looked so confused, so unsure, he leaned his crutches against the counter and opened his arms to her, offering comfort as instinctively as to one of his children. But when she blindly pressed herself against him, tucking her head under his chin, resting her forehead against his chest, all paternal feelings seared away in a flash of heat as intense as a brushfire. He felt scorched and raw, and the full impact of Cyrus's words hit him for the first time.

What if his eccentric old professor was right? What if Sara was ready to stop running? The thought, coupled with the feel of her in his arms, rocked him where he stood, and he wrapped his arms more tightly around her to steady himself. What if she spent a little more time on the ranch and decided she was through running? That she'd exorcised whatever demons had sent her on this solitary journey? He was almost afraid to consider the possibilities.

"You understand, don't you, Mac?" Sara asked, her voice muffled against him, her breath fanning warmly against his neck above the open V of his shirt.

"Of course I do." He tried to sound soothing, while at the same time his mind raced with a way to broach the subject of her staying. Because it had suddenly become vitally important to him that she stay—for just a few more days.

"Cyrus might have a point, you know," he said, loosening his grip and moving back so he could see her face. He wanted to smooth the frown that furrowed the space between her dove gray eyes. "If a couple of days here helps put things in a new light—"

She shook her head. "Mac, I won't be any different on Friday."

"Probably not," he agreed, treading carefully, barely understanding what drove him on. "But if that's true, then it shouldn't make any difference if you stayed, should it? I mean, if you really are living the way you want—"

"I am."

"If you're not just running scared—"

"I'm not."

"Then stay for the dance." He laid his thumbs against her lips as she opened her mouth to protest, a hand cupping either side of her face. She fell silent, though her lips quivered slightly, a satiny softness against his callused thumbs.

"I don't want you to leave because you're afraid to stay."

Oh, but she was afraid, Sara thought. Afraid to give any more of her heart to this man and his sons and his land. Afraid she'd already given too much. She tried to still the trembling that shivered through her at his touch.

"I'm not afraid," she lied.

"Prove it." The way his eyes darkened and flashed with challenge told her he knew she lied.

Her chin rose at the challenge. She was responding even though she was aware he was manipulating her exactly as Cyrus had. Maybe she wanted to be persuaded. Maybe she wanted to grasp at any reason to stay near him. Just a few more days... Her thoughts must have shown on her face because a small smile tugged at the corners of his mouth, a smile of triumph. He could tell she was weakening.

"Stay." He pulled her close. "You deserve some fun after all the work you've done this week. And I'd like a chance to dance with you." The trembling started again at the intimate way his belt buckle prodded her stomach, his thighs hard where they pressed against hers. She knew he felt the tremors, and his smile widened.

"You can't dance in a cast," she said. She'd meant to sound firm, but it came out soft, flirting. Like she'd already given in.

"Then stay to prop me up on the dance floor."

She squirmed from his arms, needing to put space between them, trying to maintain some dignity while she did exactly what he wanted. She reached for his crutches and handed them to him. "So I'm supposed to stay for the big dance just to prove to you and Cyrus that I can? I'm supposed to let you two shamelessly manipulate me like that?"

"Right."

"Okay."

He laughed in surprise. "Okay?"

"Okay. I give up." She put her hands on her hips and stared at him. "So now I suppose you're going to watch me every minute for some kind of sign? Waiting for me to put the spices in alphabetical order or something?"

Mac shrugged. "If you haven't changed, you haven't changed. Sara, it doesn't matter to me."

He couldn't know that was the nicest thing anyone had ever said to her.

The morning of the dance, Sara drove up the long gravel drive to Libby's house and parked in the shade of an ancient weeping willow tree. Its long branches hung to the ground, brushing the gravel layered with leaves still matted from last fall. The house was a pale tan with white trim more than ready for a fresh coat of paint. A wide porch ran along the front of the house, looking inviting and homey in spite of, or because of, the slight sag in its roof. The entire place had the look of a woman who'd just kicked off her shoes and undone her girdle and heaved a big sigh of relief.

Libby and her mother sat on the porch in front of sewing machines placed at each end of a metal table. Red checkered cloth mounded on their laps, covered the table and spilled onto the splinted floorboards.

"Morning, Sara," Libby called as she got out of her truck and started toward the two women. "Really appreciate the help. We're down to the wire here."

"I'm not much of a seamstress," she said. She walked up the porch steps and watched in admiration as Libby pressed on a foot pedal and sent the material flying through the machine, the needle pumping up and down.

"All straight seams," Libby replied. "Just something to cover up the sawhorses and plywood."

"What would you like me do?"

"How about if you start on the handwork? We're supposed to make these little gathered covers for the candle holders." Libby stood and swept a pile of checks off the table and into her arms. As soon as Sara seated herself in a nearby rocking chair, Libby dumped the material and a sample cover unceremoniously in her lap. "There you go." She dropped needle, thread, scissors and an apple-shaped pincushion on a nearby wooden table then headed to her machine.

Sara worked her hands free and reached for the spool of red thread. She'd agreed to spend the day helping the women with the last of the decorations for the dance, and then Libby and her daughter were going to "do her," as Rebecca called it. She didn't have a dress in her pared down wardrobe, nor a curling iron, nor sufficient jewelry, nor adequate makeup, nor any of the things the teenager deemed necessary for the social event of Dutch Creek's summer season. Mother and daughter had declared they had the perfect dress for her to borrow. She hadn't seen it yet, but considering the predilection of both for the outrageous she was a little hesitant about the upcoming fashion session.

"That's quite the outfit you got there," Libby's mother said, spitting out a mouthful of pins.

Still thinking about Libby's penchant for large turquoise jewelry and Rebecca's dyed hair, it took her a minute to realize Edith wasn't referring to clothes, but was nodding toward her camper.

"I like it," she said, deftly working the needle into the first piece of cloth.

"Always wanted myself one of those recreational vehicles," Edith said, pronouncing the words carefully, like a foreign language.

"Really, Mom?" Libby looked up from her machine, cornflower blue eyes wide. "I never knew that."

"Yup. A big one. With a satellite dish on top that'd pick up a whole bunch of channels and captain's chairs that swivel clear around and one of those itty-bitty refrigerators with those tiny ice cube trays." Her machine hummed to a stop and she looked at the truck in her driveway. "Must be quite a feeling to just drive off across the country...." Her voice trailed away, and after a moment the red checks once again began to flow smoothly under her hands.

Libby was obviously as surprised by her mother's words as Sara. "You'd like to do something like that?"

"Goodness, no, not anymore." Edith pushed her wire-rimmed glasses higher on her nose, all business now.

But Sara could see Libby was intrigued. "What do you mean not anymore? You *used* to want to drive off across the country?"

It was an incongruous thought. Edith Swanson looked like everyone's grandma, with her soft white curls, plump cheeks, sensible beige dress that hung modestly to mid-calf, thick ankles in sturdy brown orthopedic shoes. She looked as if she'd be at home in a kitchen, up to her elbows in apple pie and cinnamon, not at the wheel of an RV, swiveling jauntily in a captain's chair.

"There were days, 'specially when you and your brother and sisters were little—" She shrugged. "Something like that sitting in the driveway would have been pretty hard to resist."

Sara nodded, surprised to find a kindred spirit in the ranch wife. "I know what you mean."

"Well, I don't," Libby said. "Tell you the truth, Sara, I can't imagine living the way you do."

"That's 'cause you've always had choices," her mother said. "I seen to that."

"Choices?"

"In my day, we didn't have choices when it came to things like marriage and childbearing," Edith explained. "You just did it. No one expected anything else. But you—" She paused to snip a thread and tie off a seam. "You went away to college, took that trip to Spain, had yourself that fancy job for years before you got married and had Rebecca. It's the freedom to choose that makes all the difference." She looked at the truck. "Then you don't feel so much like headin' for the hills."

The women were silent, the only sound the whirl of the sewing machines. Sara found herself thinking about

Edith's words, wondering about the choices she'd made and if they'd really been her choices at all.

She'd loyally refused to give any credence to Cyrus's contention that her late husband had been in any way responsible for the tension she'd lived under for so long. So Greg had liked a neat and orderly home, too—that wasn't a crime. But she couldn't help comparing him, for just a moment, to Mac. She couldn't help wondering if, without Greg's influence, she might have gradually relaxed, loosened and softened instead of winding tighter and tighter.

After all, Mac's shirts never needed starch. Mac's schedule was a calendar thumbtacked on the wall next to the phone, and the only thing written on the white squares of June was an eye exam appointment for Jacob. Mac's flowers weren't in neat color-coordinated beds with the taller snapdragons always behind the low-growing phlox. It was remarkable to her to realize she *liked* his soft chambray shirts with the frayed collars, and the chores seemed to get done even without a schedule, and she found the chaotic profusion of roses and daisies and tiger lilies surprisingly pleasing.

But what if she planted new flowers? she demanded of herself, playing devil's advocate. Wouldn't she still make sure reds weren't near oranges? If she was ever responsible for hanging up Mac's shirts, wouldn't she insist on separating the winter weights from the summer, short sleeves from long?

She didn't know. She bit off a thread with unnecessary viciousness, forgoing the scissors. In spite of her protests that she hadn't changed, didn't want to change, that she liked her life the way it was, she'd surreptitiously found herself setting up little tests all week. After a late night snack, she'd leave the dishes in the sink to be washed the next morning. Then she'd go to her bedroom and carefully analyze how she felt about the undone chore, impatient with her childish games, yet at the same time holding her breath to see if those dishes started calling to her.

The work on the ranch was hard, physically much harder than anything she'd done in Denver, but there was none of the hectic routine, the stress she remembered from that other life. She understood that most of the pressure then had been self-imposed, the expectations had been from herself, not others, but this was such an utterly different life-style and pace, she hadn't yet found her stomach knotting into that hard core, that sick lump of nerves. Had she changed over the last two years without realizing it?

Stop it, she ordered, impatient with her thoughts. *It's only because it's someone else's house and someone else's life. That's why you can leave the dishes in the sink. The chores don't seem so overwhelming because you can leave anytime you want.* She hadn't changed, she told herself firmly. It was just a temporary aberration.

Damn! She'd been paying little attention to her work, her fingers automatically pushing and pulling the needle, and the gathers had gradually widened as she went. She reached for the scissors and began to pick out the stitches, ready to start over, to make the seam right. The scissors slipped and the sharp metal tip went under her thumbnail. A bright drop of blood immediately oozed out, smearing across the red checks as she jerked her hand from the material.

"Libby, do you have a seam ripper?" she asked. "I'm going to cut off my finger if I keep on using these scissors."

Libby didn't even look up from her machine. "Whatever you did, leave it. Nobody will mind. It'll be good enough."

Good enough? Sara looked hard at the cloth with its narrow-to-wide stitches. The drop of blood had soaked into the material, indistinguishable, a round drop of red lost in the squares. Was it really good enough? Had anything in her life ever been good enough? Could it be now? Could she live with good enough? She didn't know. She was afraid—terrified—to find out.

She put down the scissors. She twisted a new knot in the end of the thread and went on from where she'd left off, past the blood, leaving the uneven seam alone.

Chapter Eight

"Well, what do you think?" Libby shouted over the music, coming up behind Sara with two paper cups of punch. She handed one to Sara and used her free hand to gesture around the rapidly filling gym.

"I already told you, it looks marvelous," Sara assured her. "Stop worrying. Everyone seems to be having a wonderful time."

"But you can still smell the sweaty socks, can't you?"

"Hardly at all. Really."

The Dutch Creek High School gym, home of the Dutch Creek Bison, sparkled in party finery. Its hardwood floor shined with the rich, inner glow of eighty-year-old oak. The wooden bleachers on either side wore their new coat of blue paint and white trim with Bison pride. A few bricks in the walls were turning to powder from age, but they still managed to support a row of towering windows, each piece of thin glass divided into hundreds of panes by dust-catching wooden strips, reminiscent of a time when heat and labor were cheap.

Libby and her women had gone all out with decorations. The electronic scoreboard, which took up most of one wall, was shrouded in black cloth, a cosmic background to aluminum-foil-wrapped stars and moons. Silver strands streamed from the two basketball hoops, shimmering to the floor in a cascade of reflected light, swaying to the beat of invisible air currents stirred by passing couples. A row of tables, scarred sawhorse legs discreetly skirted in red and white check, were crammed with warming pots of wieners in barbecue sauce and meatballs in sour cream. Best dishes overflowed with Grandma's creamy coleslaw, baked beans and blue-ribbon potato salad. Doily-covered baking sheets bent under mounds of brownies, cookies and oozing slices of pie.

Sara surveyed the feast and tried to suck in her stomach another inch, tugging at the tight material around her hips.

"Stop that." Libby swatted at her hands. "You look great and that dress is perfect."

To her surprise, Libby's and Rebecca's choice of dress for her had been close to perfect, a simple, sleeveless black sheath, so understated, so elegant, Sara would have felt just as comfortable wearing it to the Denver Symphony as she did here in a high school gym. Unfortunately, although several inches taller, Libby had the lithe body of a long-distance runner, which forced Sara's more generous curves to hug the seams a little closer at the hips and pushed extra cleavage into the low neckline.

Still, with diamond teardrops in her ears, wispy black high heels and her hair done in a simple French twist, Sara was pleased with her appearance. But she wished the nervous flutter in her stomach would go away. It had started hours ago as she'd let the women fuss over her, dressing her with the ritualistic solemnity of some primitive culture preparing a bride for marriage—or a virgin for sacrifice. She knew it was anticipation, not for the dance, but for

Mac. She wanted him to see her like this, high heels instead of tennis shoes, perfume instead of sweat.

"Any sign of Mac yet?" Libby's voice echoed her thoughts. The blonde looked as cool as ice in blue silk. Her long hair was braided and wrapped around the crown of her head, and the dress's long, tight sleeves and high neck gave her a regal look. But the dress also had a dramatic absence of back, exposing an alarming amount of skin in a deep V that almost met the matching slit in the skirt. This mixture of fire and ice had cowboys tripping over their newly polished boots to get to her, and two were making their way toward her now, like moths to a flame.

"Maybe we shouldn't have left him alone with the boys to get ready," Libby went on. "Becky's going to go nuts if Jacob doesn't get here soon."

Sara knew how the girl felt. She scanned the crowded gym one more time, waving briefly at Cyrus and Susie where they worked harmoniously, ladling out punch into paper cups. She'd arrived early with Libby to help with last-minute fussing. Every time the heavy doors had swung open, her head would swivel to see if the cowboy coming through it had Mac's dark hair, his deep blue eyes, his wide shoulders thrown back in that way that announced a man had entered the room—and the room had damned well better know it.

"Oh, here they come." Libby smiled an apology at the two cowboys who were headed her way and hurried across the gym, dodging swaying couples.

Sara's heart skidded sideways at the sight of Mac standing in the doorway. His crutches seemed such a part of him by now, they didn't detract a bit from his western-cut suit, charcoal gray over an immaculate white shirt. His ever-present hat was nowhere to be seen, and Sara loved the way his hair curled at his nape and around his ears as if still pressed by the weight of it.

She saw Libby say something to Jacob before pointing in the direction of the punch bowl where her daughter stood with a group of teenagers. Jacob grinned in reply and headed that way, Michael tagging along behind him. Then Mac leaned down and asked her something. Libby turned and held out a finger, pointing directly at Sara. Mac raised his eyes and they met hers. Electricity jumped across the length of the gymnasium. As he moved toward her, the crowd disappeared, the loud music dimmed to insignificance, the lights faded until the only thing she saw was Mac.

His eyes never left hers.

The music switched to something slow and crooning. He stopped in front of her. He put both crutches in one hand and held them out to a man passing by. "Set these over by the wall, would you, Bruce?"

The startled cowboy took the crutches with a murmur of confused agreement she barely heard. She shifted into Mac's arms and they began to sway in place, eyes locked.

"Sorry I'm late. I forgot the pants to this suit wouldn't fit over the cast. I had to rip the seam myself."

Sara glanced at the expensive material, neatly pinned around the cast, which looked like it had received a good scrubbing. "I never thought of that, either. I'll sew them tomorrow morning before I go."

A muscle twitched near Mac's eye, as if in a response to a sudden stab of pain. "Don't."

"What?"

"Don't talk about leaving. Not tonight." He pulled her closer and they danced silently for a moment, unmoving as the north star while constellations of bright couples rotated around them. "I missed you today," he said quietly, his breath nuzzling her ear.

"Was everything okay? You found the sandwiches I left for lunch? And the casserole for supper?"

His look silenced her. "I didn't say I missed your cooking. I said I missed you."

She swallowed hard.

"You look beautiful," he murmured. "Stunning."

"Thank you." She tried to calm the thudding of her heart, searching for some innocuous topic that would take her mind off the sensations Mac's touch, voice, scent created inside her. "It's certainly a change from jeans. It feels good, too. I'd forgotten the tingle you get from getting all dressed up for a big night. And I'd forgotten how good it feels to work on a community project like this—the satisfaction." She smiled at him. "These two weeks have really been a wonderful time for me, Mac."

"For me, too." His smile was bittersweet. "But you didn't find what you're looking for here, did you? We flunked the test." It was the first time all week he'd referred to the challenge he and Cyrus had offered, the test to see if she was ready to rejoin their idea of the real world. It was the first time he'd let on that the results were important to him, too.

Her smile faltered. "It was my test," she said, "not yours. I flunked, not you."

"You seemed relaxed this week. I thought maybe—" He shrugged. "I thought you were happy here."

"I was! I was very happy."

"But?"

She struggled to find the words to make him understand. To make him understand that she would leave even if it meant she'd live with this ache inside her for the rest of her life. "Mac," she said, "what are your dreams? What is it you want more than anything in the world?"

He didn't hesitate. "I want my sons to grow up healthy and happy, and I want the ranch to prosper."

"And what could I do or say that would change that?"

He was quiet, his eyes fixed on some distant point over

her head. The lines around his mouth suddenly seemed more pronounced, the crease between his eyes deeper. His voice was rough as he agreed, "Dreams aren't that easy to let go of, are they?"

"Not when you've fought for them for so long. Not when they're the only things that have kept you sane."

The silence was longer this time. He continued to stare past her, and she could almost see him begin to disconnect, withdraw. "So you're leaving tomorrow?"

"I packed this morning before I went over to Libby's."

"Still headed north?"

She nodded. "I think so. But maybe I'll be able to swing down this way again sometime this fall." She knew her words made it worse, knew the promise of seeing him again someday just prolonged the agony, yet she was unable to keep from giving herself some tiny hope. "I'll try to stop in and say hi."

"That would be nice," he said politely. Finally he lowered his gaze to meet hers, his eyes dark and unfathomable. "Maybe someday you'll dream a new dream."

She nodded again, her throat too tight to speak, eyes wide open, afraid to blink lest tears spill over.

In spite of his controlled words and remote look, he clutched her so close she molded against him on the dance floor. They held each other, her head on his shoulder, one of his arms around her waist, the other cradling her hand between them, pressed over his heart. She was vaguely aware of the curious glances of other dancers as they moved past, but she didn't care. She didn't want him to ever let her go.

The music ended. The sudden swell of voices seemed shrill, the lights bright, the crowd pressing, the smell of food cloying. She took a deep breath and forced herself to take a step away from Mac. The separation chilled her, but she knew she couldn't remain in the magic circle of his arms any longer.

Just then Libby walked past on the arm of a short, balding man sporting the beginnings of a paunch. A bolo tie with an enormous turquoise rock was centered below his Adam's apple.

"Libby looks wonderful tonight, doesn't she?" she asked, desperately trying to force their conversation toward something less intimate, less painful.

"Yeah," Mac agreed. He wanted to be distracted as much as Sara seemed to want him to be. He wanted to stop smelling roses every waking minute—and in his dreams, too. He wanted to stop craving smoky eyes and soft skin, silky hair and sweet, light laughter. He made himself look at Libby where she stood with the mayor of Dutch Creek. The old goat had his hand down low on Libby's bare back, and sweat beaded heavily on his exposed forehead.

Mac had to smile at that. Libby could have that effect on a man, he thought. She looked great, as always. They'd dated for awhile in high school, but there'd never been any sparks there. He watched her laugh politely at something the mayor said. He frowned.

Now there was the type of woman he should be interested in, he told himself firmly. She was a good friend, familiar with his world, a hard worker. She'd be a wonderful helpmate at the ranch. And she was loyal. Look at the way she'd come home to help her parents. She'd stick by him and the boys through thick and thin. Down to earth. Cheerful. There'd be no traipsing across the country trying to find herself. Definitely, Libby was just right for him.

Somebody put in another CD, something loud and raucous and young. He sighed and gathered Sara into his arms again, where she fit like she was a part of him. They began to sway, ignoring the beat of the music. He laid his cheek against her hair, breathing deep to capture the smell of roses, willing himself to remember it, because soon, too soon, she would leave and take his heart with her.

Sara slammed the camper door with a solid, metallic thunk. She'd taken the last of her clothes from the scented walnut dresser in the guest bedroom and crammed them into the narrow drawers under the Formica table in the camper. Her shampoo was in the wire basket that hung from the shower head, her three pair of shoes once again took up a complete shelf in the closet, and her purse sat exactly between the seat belt fasteners in the middle of the front seat.

She was ready.

She turned to look at the house, rosy in the early morning light wherever the tall cottonwoods let the sun stream through. Dew sparkled on the grass, highlighting individual blades, and the air smelled clean and cool and expectant. She walked up the porch steps, trailing her fingers along the rail, savoring the feel of the warming wood. Slowly, she pulled open the wide front door and entered the living room.

There was no sound coming from behind the closed doors upstairs. She was surprised the boys weren't up yet, since they'd left the dance with a group of their friends hours before she'd been able to tear herself away from Mac. By the time she'd arrived home, they were already in bed and snores had been audible from one end of the hall to the other.

She found herself touching things as she passed through the room. She ran her hand along the back of the chair Mac always sat in to read the paper. She fingered a vase of cosmos on the hall table, stroking a delicate lavender petal. She carefully traced the outline of each face in the family photograph on the wall.

She'd never said goodbye to her own things this way. The only sentiment she could remember came closer to good riddance. Briefly, she allowed herself to wonder what it would be like if she wasn't saying goodbye. If she lived on a ranch like this, like the one she used to imagine for herself all those years ago, if she went back to college, got her degree, became a vet—

She turned her back on the photograph. Enough of that. Time to get breakfast. The men would be down soon, and she wanted to make sure they had a good meal before she left. But as she walked determinedly through the kitchen, her eye caught the cabinet full of salt and pepper shakers, the windmills and kittens and cars, so lovingly collected for so many years. She crossed the room and stood in front of the glass doors, studying each piece.

A little black-and-white cow stood off to one side, with a pink udder, ridiculously long eyelashes and a silly cow smile. Carefully, she turned the intricate key in the lock, swung the door open and picked up the porcelain figurine. Hairline cracks in the glaze revealed its age, and a thin ribbon of glue on one of its hind legs marked where a break had been painstakingly mended. She smiled at its whimsical expression, said a mental goodbye to the figures she had already dusted twice in the time she'd been there and went to replace the cow on its glass shelf. As its feet touched the glass, the hind leg broke off, neatly following the old glue joint.

Damn. She gathered up the pieces. She'd have to fix it before she left. She remembered why she'd been so happy to sell her doodads and knickknacks, all the little chunks of glass and porcelain from the shelves of her other life.

She laid the cow and its leg on the counter next to the refrigerator and began to pull out eggs, bacon, butter and bread. For someone who hated to cook, she took unexpected pleasure in preparing this last meal. The smell of sizzling bacon mingled with the aroma of fresh coffee had to be one of the unparalleled experiences in life, she thought, laying strips on a paper towel to drain.

She heard footsteps behind her. "I'm afraid the boys won't be needing any breakfast," Mac said, picking up a piece of bacon with his fingers. "We seem to have a little problem."

He jerked his head in the direction of the boys who shuffled in behind him, placing their feet slowly and carefully, one in front of the other.

"What in heaven's name?" She stared at the pair, noting the matching greenish tints to their skin. Jacob's hair was a tangled matt on one side, and the expression in his eyes told her even the thought of a comb was painful. Michael's top lip stuck dryly to the dull metal of his braces, and his mouth hung open as if he couldn't summon the strength to close it.

"The flu?" she asked, reaching out to place a hand against Michael's clammy forehead.

"They wish," Mac growled with no trace of sympathy. "It turns out they and their friends thought this was a good year to sample Susie's punch."

"Oh, no!" She shuddered at the memory of the spiked drink the cowboys at the dance had swilled with such gusto. A few sips from a paper cup had sent her head spinning and she'd dumped the rest in the ladies' room. "Did they know?"

"You bet they knew." He took another piece of bacon from the plate, and the boys blanched as they watched him tear off an end from the greasy strip. "It's too bad Saturday's the busiest day at the station, Jacob," he said, chewing slowly, with exaggerated relish. "That bell ringing whenever a car pulls up is going to make your head fall off your shoulders. And Michael, the smell of Justice's stall will set real good on that stomach of yours—especially on a hot day like today, when the manure is steaming and ripe.''

Both boys bolted down the hall toward the bathroom.

"That wasn't very nice," Sara said, pushing away his hand as he reached for another slice of bacon.

"I don't feel nice. I feel mad as hell." He dropped into a chair and let his crutches clatter to the floor.

"Has this ever happened before?"

Mac shook his head. "First time. But I should have expected something like this. They're at that age where they like to push the boundaries. I should have been keeping an eye on them but I—we—"

Sara knew what he meant. They'd been so wrapped up in each other last night, Michael and Jacob were the last thing on their minds. When the boys came to the kitchen, even whiter than before, she felt guilt curl inside her. They could have drunk the whole damn punchbowl and she would have never noticed.

"We're really, really sorry, Dad," Michael said, his eyes fixed firmly on the hole in the toe of his sock.

"Enough. I heard it all upstairs." Mac glared at them, but they wouldn't meet his eyes. They looked young and miserable and utterly ill.

"Ah, hell, get back to bed, both of you," he said with an exasperated shooing motion. "You'll be worthless till noon anyway. I'll take care of things myself this morning." He frowned, his mind obviously jumping ahead to the huge amount of work to be done. "I've got to feed the animals first. The station will have to stay closed till I can get down there later on."

Mac looked as miserable as his sons, and Sara felt pity mix with her guilt. She heard herself saying, "Why don't I work the station for an hour or two this morning while you do the chores?"

Mac was shaking his head even before she'd finished speaking. "I don't want to keep you."

Her stomach clenched at his polite, impersonal tone, as if last night was already something to be tucked away in some old photo album. She waved aside his objections, keeping her voice businesslike. "A couple of hours. It's no big deal."

"Just till I get 'em fed and the stalls mucked?"

"Sure."

Relief was obvious in his face. He turned to the boys. "What are you two doing standing there? Get to bed. And I'd forget about any big plans you might have for the rest of the summer," he called after them. "This grounding's going to be measured in months, not days."

Mac bolted down his breakfast and left for the barn while she cleaned the kitchen. She found herself taking extra care with every little chore. She wanted things to be just right when she left—not from some compulsive need for order, but as a small way to make things easier on the men who had come to mean so much to her.

When the kitchen was in order, she picked up the broken salt shaker, slammed the screen door behind her and crossed the lawn toward the gravel drive that led to the gas station near the highway. The drive passed near the garden, now neatly weeded, the corn knee high, the zucchini almost ready to bear. She hoped the men could find someone to can the tomatoes for them this year, noticing the vines loaded with small green globes.

She frowned as she moved past the strawberry bed. Their normally dark green leaves had turned brown on the edges and drooped forlornly. She tucked the cow in the pocket of her blouse and leaned over to pull up a plant. A snap of the thin root revealed the telltale reddish color inside. Although the scientific name eluded her, she knew there was no cure for the fungus attacking the roots. Mac might as well pull them all up now and move the bed to a new spot. Damn. She'd have to remember to tell him about it before she left.

Mac flung another pitchfork full of stinking wood shavings into the wheelbarrow, growing angrier by the minute. Every forkful was a challenge as he tried to keep his balance, his weight on his good foot, his cast barely resting on the ground. Dusty shavings had managed to work their way deep down inside the cast and had started an itch that crawled around where he couldn't scratch.

"How could they do something so totally stupid," he fumed, addressing the horse that stood patiently in the shadows. He leaned on the pitchfork to rest, drawing deep breaths of acrid air while sweat trickled down his back, starting an itch there, too. He hadn't mucked a stall in months, and never in a cast. Damn the boys, anyway.

But his anger and disappointment were mixed with the new, uneasy realization that he'd grown dependent on his sons' help with the ranch as they'd gotten older. He needed them. And that thought brought an additional worry as he envisioned the teenage rebellion and peer pressure waiting to fall on his family like a ton of bricks. He had a sinking feeling last night was just the beginning of the problems he was going to face as a parent. A single parent.

He left the wheelbarrow where it stood. There was no way he could move it with a full load. One of the boys would have to do it later. He swore. "What do you think of that, Justice? Did you ever think you'd see the day when I couldn't move a load of horse—"

The gelding's nicker cut him off. The horse drew back his lips and shook his head, seeming to laugh at Mac's predicament.

"Oh, shut up," he muttered. An hour had passed since breakfast, and he wasn't even half through with the animals. He swore some more as he spread fresh shavings on the hard-packed dirt floor, more apprehensive about the handicap of his cast than at any time since the accident.

His mind skirted the thought of Sara and how dependent they'd all become on her. In such a very short time, she'd become integral to their lives. How were they going to manage without her? How was he going to face those long, quiet summer evenings without her beside him on the porch? How was he going to take pleasure in riding out to check on his herd without her beside him, ordering him to slow Justice down so her little mare could keep up? Why in the hell did he all of a sudden need everybody?

He led the horse into the clean stall and patted his smooth neck. "What are we going to do without her, huh, boy?" He slumped down on a bale of straw. Pulling out a stiff yellow stem, he worked it inside the cast, wiggling the piece of straw this way and that, trying to reach the itch. Glumly, he wondered if there was a can of tuna anywhere he could open for supper tonight.

"Do you hear that, Edith?" Sara asked Libby's mother as she rang up her sale—eight gallons of unleaded—and handed her the change.

"That bangin'?" The woman dropped the coins into the bottom of her shiny black handbag and snapped it shut.

"And that sort of moan. Real low?"

Edith cocked her head and listened. "Doesn't sound good. What is it?"

"I think it's the freezer." She slammed the cash register shut and moved quickly from behind the counter to the freezer next to the soda pop case. The old machine clanged again, then groaned and gave a shimmying shudder. She slid back the glass lid and peered inside as if the ice cream bars and little cups of frozen yogurt could tell her what was the matter.

"It's smoking," Edith said calmly, peering over her shoulder.

"You think so? Maybe it's just the cool air mixing with the warm."

"Looks like smoke to me."

Sara ran her hand across the front of the case and around the sides. The metal felt warm, hot, really hot.

"Uh-oh. I think I'd better unplug it." The wrenching noises stopped abruptly as she tugged the cord from the socket. She looked at the limp cord in her hand and sighed. "First the cow, then the strawberries and now the freezer. I'm going to have to make a list of all this stuff for Mac before I go."

She helped herself to a fudge-caramel bar covered with nuts and held the lid open for Edith. "Take your pick. They're not going to stay hard for long."

"Don't mind if I do." The woman chose a low-fat yogurt bar and tore off the wrapper. "So you're moving on?"

Sara nodded.

Edith nodded, too, quiet for a moment while she licked at the pink concoction on her stick. "Saw you and Mac at the dance last night. I thought—"

"No," Sara interrupted too quickly. "I'm leaving for Yellowstone just as soon as Mac finishes the chores this morning."

"Um." Edith looked as if she wanted to say more but decided against it. "What's all this about cows and strawberries?" she asked instead.

Sara filled her in on the morning's problems as she returned to her post by the cash register. "So now I've got to get this cow back together before I go." She threw her half-melted ice-cream bar into the trash and picked up the two pieces of the little shaker from the glass counter. As she fingered the porcelain figurine, a feeling of déjà vu swept over her, so immediate, so powerful, it was nearly overwhelming.

"What's the matter, child? You look like you saw a ghost."

"I guess I did." She shook her head to clear it, shrugging off the disturbing time shift. "I've done all this so many times before, that's all."

"You've fixed salt shakers before?"

She smiled at the woman's confused expression. "Something close to it, anyway. I can't tell you how often I've worked over some shattered keepsake, trying to repair a possession that owned me more than I owned it. Or the times some appliance broke down, leaving me with the mess to clean, the repairman to call, the insurance policy to find. And that lawn. Edith, you can't imagine how I worried over that lawn. Dollar-spot disease or melting-out disease? I cared—I cared so *desperately* which."

She laughed hollowly. "And now I've got cows and strawberries and melting ice cream—"

"But Sara," Edith interrupted, the confused frown between her brows even deeper, "these are Mac's problems. Not yours."

She jumped slightly, startled. "That's right. Of course they are. I— It just reminded me, that's all."

"Oh." The woman gave her a strange look then tucked her purse under her arm. "Well, I guess I better be going. Carl will be wondering where I got off to. Thanks for the ice cream."

"You bet."

Edith pulled open the door. "Sara?" She stopped in the doorway. "I worry about my lawn, too, you know. It's okay to care. As long as you get to choose what you care about."

Sara watched her get into her car, pull away from the gas pumps and turn onto the highway. Choices again. Stay or go. Ranch or Yellowstone. Dreams or—love? What if the choices were too hard to make? she wanted to shout after the departing car. What if she cared about it all?

She forced herself to turn her attention to the pieces she held in her hand. She reached for a tube of glue and squeezed a drop onto the detached leg. Carefully, she fitted the two pieces together and held them in place between her fingers.

Unmoving, she sat on the stool and waited. Her toes began to tap an impatient little rhythm. She glanced at her watch, suddenly restless. It was time to go. The goodbyes had been said. The wound had been inflicted. It was time to run away and hide, lick all the sore places and let the healing process begin. Let time and distance mercifully fade Mac and his sons and his ranch into just another wonderful, if bittersweet, memory. She ignored the little inner voice that said there wasn't enough time or distance on earth to make that happen.

She shifted on the stool, antsier by the second. Her fingers grew numb as she held the sharp edges together. An engine roared past outside, and she glanced up to look out the window. A pickup, pulling a long, silver trailer as sleek and streamlined as a shark, whizzed past. It disappeared before she could blink, before she could see the people inside the truck—people without wilting strawberries, melting ice cream or broken cows.

She slid from the stool and stood, leaning her weight from one foot to the other as she held her hand perfectly still on the counter. She looked at her watch again, desperate, suddenly, to move. A car pulled up, making the bell over the doorway ring. Enough was enough. It was time. Slowly, she began to ease her fingers apart.

The door swung open, setting off the bell again. She opened her fingers.

"Hi, Mom!"

The leg fell off in her hand.

Chapter Nine

"Laura!" She stared as her daughter walked into the station.

"Surprised?"

"Of course I'm surprised. What are you doing here?"

Laura pushed oversize sunglasses onto her head, revealing the intense brown eyes of her father. Twenty-four years old, she had his straight nose and light brown hair, which she'd streaked with blond highlights and kept short and tightly curled. She wore denim shorts, a crisp red blouse and white leather sandals that revealed carefully manicured and polished toenails.

"I had a couple days off work so I thought I'd run up and take a look at the place that could keep my mother off the road for two whole weeks. Thought maybe I could learn their secret."

She smiled, but her voice had an edge that immediately put Sara on alert. Something was going on here. When she'd left Denver, Laura had made a point of not saying goodbye, an example of the passive hostility she'd perfected to an art. She wouldn't drive halfway across Wyoming on a whim.

"No secret," Sara replied carefully. "The Wallaces needed some help for a little while and I happened to be in the right place at the right time."

"The Wallaces? Or one Wallace in particular?" Again the smile that didn't hide the underlying tension in her eyes.

"Can I get you a soda or something? Why don't you sit down and we can talk. I like the way you're wearing your hair." She tried to change the subject, but Laura would have none of it.

"What gives, Mother?"

"I told you all about this on the phone the other night." She kept her voice calm and matter-of-fact, realizing her daughter was as tightly coiled as a spring. The jagged porcelain edge she'd forgotten she still held began to press uncomfortably into her palm. She laid the leg down and once again busied herself with the glue, fitting the edges together, resigned, waiting for the explosion. She'd seen Laura like this before and knew there was no way to head it off.

"Not *all* about it, Mother. Although in your three phone calls, I did hear *all* about some guy named Mac. More than I wanted to know, to tell you the truth." She moved closer to lean a hip against the counter, pretending to watch Sara repair the figurine.

She could see the slight tremble in her daughter's hands and wondered how many cups of coffee she'd had on the drive up from Denver that morning.

"So," Laura said with studied nonchalance, "you guys doing it?"

Sara's head snapped up. "That's enough, Laura!"

"Really?" She laughed, a strained, unattractive sound. "There has to be some reason you can stay here for two weeks, but I can't get you to spend more than a day or so with me. And poor Grandma barely gets a weekend now and then.''

"I told you. They needed—"

"Well, maybe I've needed you, too!"

"And I've given, Laura!" The anger spurted before she could control it. "And given and given and given. And you and your father were only too happy to take whatever I had to give. *Everything* I had to give. There's a difference between needing and wanting!"

Laura looked stricken, her face blanching, her eyes large and luminous, childlike in their hurt. Sara immediately regretted her words. She'd heard the same harangue from her daughter for the last two years, but seldom—never— answered back. She was sorry she'd done so this time.

"Let's not do this again," she pleaded. "Look, why don't you have a Popsicle. The freezer's broken and they're melting all over the place."

"No, thank you," Laura said stiffly.

"Laura, please—"

"It's okay." Laura made a hands-off gesture, palms outward. "I never realized Dad and I had been such a burden to you."

"You weren't a burden. Now stop this before you make yourself sick. Have you been taking those new allergy pills the doctor gave you?"

"Thanks for the concern, but I've managed to take care of myself for quite awhile now."

Sara sighed and closed her eyes briefly. "Did you drive all this way up here just to fight with me?"

"Actually, I thought maybe I could get you to listen to reason this time, that's all. I should have known better."

Sara prickled again but bit her tongue with an effort. Their relationship hadn't always been this way. When Laura was a child, they'd been close. The combination of her asthma and being an only child had perhaps made them too close, but Laura had shown no signs of being overly dependent. She'd been thrilled to leave home to attend the university in Fort Collins.

Her father's death during her third year at college had been devastating for her, Sara knew. In fact, that was the reason she'd stuck out two more nightmare years in the house that had felt so much like a jail. She'd wanted Laura to have that stability to fall back on during such a difficult time. She'd dutifully waited until Laura had graduated, had a good job, an apartment of her own. All the trappings of independence. When she'd driven away that summer day, she'd confidently thought she'd raised her daughter, done her part.

But Laura had never understood, and Sara knew her daughter's resentment had deepened with every mile she traveled.

"You're tired," she said, trying again. "You must have left Denver at the crack of dawn. Why don't you sit down and—"

"No, I don't think so." Laura stepped away from the counter. "In fact, I think I'll just head home. I'll let you get back to your needy Wallaces."

"They don't need me anymore," Sara said, wincing inside as she said it. "I'm leaving today—in an hour or so. I'll spend the night in Yellowstone."

"Ah, so they couldn't keep you, either? It's not just me, then?" That tense smile again that wrenched at Sara's stomach. "That's good. I was beginning to think it was something personal."

Sara stared at her daughter, helpless to stop what was happening between them. She placed the little cow on the counter where it once again stood sturdily on all four legs, and wished there was some magic glue that could help her daughter stand, as well. There was no way she could give Laura what she thought she was missing.

"I'll be back in Denver the first of September," she said instead.

"Be sure to stop by."

"Quit that," she said with an exasperated frown, having taken almost all she could stand of Laura's relentless sarcasm. "Of course I'll stop by. We'll go out to dinner and maybe shopping. My wardrobe's gotten a little sparse even for me."

"Okay." Laura pulled her sunglasses down, hiding her eyes. She hesitated, and Sara tensed. "You know, Mom, that apartment building next to me? The one you've always liked? It's being converted to condos."

"Uh-huh." Sara braced for what she knew was about to come.

"You've always said you really, really liked those apartments. And I was thinking you might want to have a permanent place, for when you're ready to come back home?"

"Oh. Well—"

"I mean, you're getting awfully old to keep up this vagabond stuff. Sooner or later you're going to want to start acting your age—"

"Excuse me?"

"Acting like a real mother again, is what I mean."

"A real mother?"

"Now, I don't mean it that way, but you have to admit you've been pretty self-centered these last two years."

That did it. She'd had enough. She was in no mood for this lecture. Not today, when her nerves were already raw. She felt the eruption swell inside her, and for once didn't try to squash it down.

"You're damn right I've been self-centered. And guess what, Laura?" She laid her palms flat on the counter and leaned toward her daughter, staring into the blank lenses of her sunglasses. "I deserve it! I spent twenty-some years spoiling you and your father rotten. Now I'm going to spend a few years—" she threw up her hands "—hell, maybe the rest of my life, centered on me! Me!"

Mac heard the raised voices even before he entered the back door of the garage. He hurried across the oil-stained floor of the garage toward the office, reacting to the pain he heard in Sara's voice. Swinging into the open doorway, he stopped when he caught sight of the other woman in the room. She looked enough like Sara, he knew immediately she must be her daughter. And it was also apparent she was very upset. In fact, she seemed to be struggling to draw a breath.

He started toward her, but Sara was already there, around the counter in a flash.

"Where's your inhaler?"

The young woman yanked off her sunglasses and began to dig frantically through the floppy brown handbag she had slung over one shoulder. Sara pulled it from her and unceremoniously dumped the contents on the counter. Keys, coins, pens, tubes of lipstick rolled across the glass top and dropped to the floor. Sweeping aside the wadded tissue and crumpled receipts, Sara found the small blue plastic cylinder she was looking for and pressed it into her daughter's hand.

The young woman placed the tube to her mouth and squeezed, drawing in air with a whistling sound that made Mac take a deep breath of his own, as if he could help force the air into her lungs.

Sara guided her to a chair against the wall and cradled her head to her shoulder, rocking her gently while they waited for the medicine to take effect.

"Is there anything I can do?" he asked quietly.

"Thanks, Mac. She'll be fine in a minute."

Her breath did seem to come easier, and color slowly seeped into her cheeks. But her eyes remained wide and frightened, and she clung to her mother while Sara's fingers rhythmically soothed the hair from her forehead.

He found the young woman watching him, and he stared back. After a moment, she raised a hand to her mouth and coughed several times. "Well, he's certainly handsome enough," she said between coughs. "I say go for it, Mom."

Sara laughed, and Mac was pleased to see some of the tension go out of her. The look she gave her daughter shined with love for the girl, and he had to admit she looked sweet with her head on her mother's shoulder, tired and young and very vulnerable. Mac had been prepared to dislike this daughter who'd given Sara so much grief, but he found himself smiling.

"Mac Wallace, this is my daughter, Laura Shepherd."

"Pleased to meet you." He balanced on one foot so he could hold out his hand to shake hers, a hand he found still clammy with sweat.

Laura drew a deep breath. "Well," she said, "this little visit didn't work out quite like I'd planned." She got shakily to her feet and began to gather up the things that had spilled from her purse.

"Let's go up to the house and have a cup of coffee," Sara said as she picked up coins that had rolled to the floor. "We can talk some more."

Laura shook her head. "I better get going. It's a long drive."

"But you just got here." Sara's concern was evident. "Stay for a while until you feel better. You shouldn't drive right now."

"I'm okay." She slipped on her sunglasses again and levered her purse over her shoulder. She smiled at Mac. "Nice to meet you, Mr. Wallace."

Mac smiled in return, watching from the sidelines, not understanding the undercurrents of emotion still so close to the surface in both women.

Laura paused at the door. She pulled her lower lip between her teeth. "I take it you don't want to put a down payment on one of the condos?"

Sara shook her head. "I don't think so."

"Come home?"

"I can't."

"Right." Laura nodded briskly. "I'll see you in September then." The bell chimed discordantly as she walked out the door.

Mac watched the shiny red car turn onto the highway, spurting gravel under its tires. "This has been one hell of a day for us parents," he said with a gusty sigh.

When Sara didn't reply, he turned to find her still sitting in the chair, her face in her hands, sobbing silently.

"Damn," he swore under his breath. He dropped into the chair her daughter had just left and pulled her close. She laid her head on his shoulder and cried without making a sound, but her whole body shook with the effort to hold back the sobs.

"There now. Hush now," he crooned. He pushed the bangs from her forehead the way she'd done to Laura, and tried to brush away the tears that streamed down her cheeks, but she turned her face toward his chest, burying it from his sight.

He let her cry. He patted her back the way he'd done when the boys had been little and ran to him with a scraped shin or bruised feelings. He said nothing, just waited quietly until her shoulders quit heaving and her tears dried to sniffles and she finally lifted her head.

Straightening, she wiped her face on her arm and rubbed

at her eyes with the heels of her hands. "So now you know what a terrible mother I am." She sniffed.

"You're not a terrible mother."

"Yes, I am. Now I am, anyway." She fished in the pocket of her jeans and pulled out a tissue to wipe her eyes again and blow her nose. "But I was a *terrific* mother for twenty-two years, and that doesn't seem to count for anything. She doesn't care how miserable I was before."

"Of course not. Kids only see their parents as parents, not as people."

"Don't I have the right to live the way I want? After all these years?"

"Of course you do."

"I mean, what does she want from me? She's twenty-four years old and making her own way in the world. She doesn't need me anymore. What does she think I'd do all day stuck in some condo in Denver?"

Mac knew these were rhetorical questions, so he didn't try to answer, just let the words tumble out, content to be her sounding board.

"Was I supposed to keep her childhood home some kind of shrine?" She talked faster, waving the soggy tissue for emphasis. "I'm supposed to be this wind-up doll that comes to life whenever she opens the door, tray of cookies in hand? Did my life end when hers began?"

She paused, as if expecting an answer.

"Of course it didn't."

"That's right. And if I want to drive around in *circles*, isn't that my business?"

He nodded.

"*This* is my life now, and I like it. Living on a ranch was just a silly childhood dream. I don't *want* to be a vet."

Surprise jolted Mac. "I didn't even know you were considering it."

"I'm not!" She practically shouted the words at him. "That part of my life is as dead as my life with Greg."

"Okay." He blinked at her vehemence. Would she really deny something with such passion if she hadn't been struggling with it? He felt a stirring of hope.

"I'm going to go to Yellowstone and Canada and I'm going to have a wonderful time."

He continued to agree with her although doing so cut to the quick. The more she vowed she was going to leave—this very minute, in fact—the more sure he became that he could convince her to stay. And he knew he'd be crazy if he did. Sara would leave him sooner or later, and when she did, he'd be left with his ranch and his sons—and the unthinkable truth that it wasn't enough anymore.

She might not be the right woman for him, might be the antithesis of the kind of woman he needed, but he wanted her desperately. So desperately it was like the ache of a broken bone, but every bone in his body must be broken, because this dull pain reached into every crook and crevasse of his body. He needed time to find a way to stop the pain. He needed her with him until he found a cure. Just a little while longer.

"Well," she said, "if everything I'm doing is so right, why do I feel so bad?" The gray eyes that stared into his were soft and liquid and forlorn. Her lips shook and he couldn't think of any way to stop the heart-wrenching tremors except to cover them with his own.

Sara melted into his arms. It was where she'd wanted to be for so long, she didn't hesitate for a moment. Where before his hands on her back had been comforting, now they moved with a sensual pressure that had her moaning against his lips. As her lips parted to release the primitive sound, his tongue swept inside, meeting hers in an intimate caress.

She ran her hands over his face, memorizing the strong

lines of his jaw, the planes of his cheekbones, the feel of his hair as it slid through her fingers. She pressed closer, wanting more of him, wanting all of him. When his mouth left hers to move along her neck, she tilted her head to ease his way. She wanted to feel his lips everywhere at once, to have his breath warm every inch of her skin, to guide his touch to every part of her.

"Stay with me," he breathed as his teeth pulled on the sensitive lobe of her ear.

Her breath caught, as much from the exquisite sensation as from his words. She tried to focus her thoughts. "There's no dance, no branding, no more broken bones, no reason—"

"No, I mean stay with me." He pulled back and his eyes reflected her arousal. "Don't go," he repeated.

His words splashed over her like ice water. She sat up and tugged at the shirt his feverish hands had mussed.

"But I have to." It was the same answer she'd just given Laura. The answer she'd given for the last two years. "Why?"

She looked into his eyes, reading emotions as confused as her own. Why? How could she explain the fear that had gnawed at her ever since she'd realized she was falling in love with Mac? Because that was what had happened. She loved him with all her heart. And still she couldn't stay.

"I flunked the test, remember?" She tried to smile.

"Forget the test! This is bigger than whether or not you squeeze the toothpaste tube in the middle or the bottom. We can work around that."

She shook her head and tried to put her fears into words. "What if the chains start to form again, Mac? I couldn't stand it." Didn't he understand? What if, a few years from now when their passion had cooled, the dishes, the dusting, the laundry, the endless routine, the crushing need to do it all perfectly, combined to stifle her until she wanted nothing more than to run away again?

"I can't do it again, Mac. I'm scared."

"And I'm not?" he asked incredulously, the beginnings of anger coloring his words. "I'm the one who'd get walked out on, you know. Again. It would be my boys who'd be hurt." He ran a hand over his face and raked it through his hair, then took her by the shoulders. "Look, we need some more time to straighten this out. How about if I come with you to Yellowstone?"

"No!" Her reaction was automatic and instinctive.

"Why not?" he demanded, his voice harsh, the anger growing.

"You can't just leave the boys and the ranch—" She stopped. How could she explain that Yellowstone had always been part of her solitary travel plans, part of that inner goal of seeing the country unencumbered, unattached, gloriously alone. To take Mac with her, to share that part of her dream, would be to admit the dream was over. Something she was too frightened to do. He shouldn't ask it of her.

"Why not?" he repeated, but his voice was cooler now, his eyes colder, wary.

"I—" How could she say he wasn't part of her dream when he was all she dreamed about?

The silence stretched between them until Mac exploded, "Damn it, Sara, you can't go!"

She was rocked by his abrupt tone and found herself withdrawing, curling inward at the note of command. No one had given her an order in a long, long time.

"You want to stay. I know you do. You couldn't kiss me like that, react like that, if you didn't want—" He broke off in frustration. "If I could just talk some *sense* into you."

She went very still inside. Coming on top of Laura's

accusations, she didn't need anyone else's criticism, anyone else pushing at her, pulling at her, telling her how to behave.

"I'm feeling perfectly sensible, thank you very much." She said it very, very quietly.

"It's sensible to run like a rabbit at the thought of commitment? Responsibility? A relationship? Hell, Sara, that's what life's all about. I need—"

"Stop!" She wanted to put her hands over her ears. "Just stop." It was starting already. The demands. The pressure. The endless needs. Her stomach clenched and the taste of acid bit at the back of her throat. She couldn't do it. She couldn't.

"I see." He dropped his hands from her. "Fine. Forget it. But at least be honest with yourself and with me. It's not some old obsession, is it? It's not the work or ranch life. It's me, isn't it?"

"No! Mac, no! It's me!"

"Hey, I've heard it before. Ronda used that same excuse. It was all too much for her, she said. But guess where my ex-wife ended up less than a year after the divorce?"

Sara looked at him, as helpless to stop his pain as she'd been her daughter's.

"She left her apartment in Cheyenne and married another rancher."

"What?"

"A rancher with a spread just as big as mine, even more isolated and nearly bankrupt to boot. And she's already got three more kids, after it took me years to convince her to have Jacob."

Sara forced herself to meet eyes dark and sore as a bruise.

"Last time I saw her, her hair was turning gray, the sun was ruining her skin, and her hands were red as lobsters from all the hard work." He smiled grimly. "But her eyes sparkled like they never did for me in all the years we were married. She was happy—happy to work her fingers to the bone for another man. But not for me. It was just me she didn't want.

"So don't give me some bull about it being the life-style you can't handle." He lifted himself to his feet and swung away from her, moving to stand behind the counter. "Go. Go on, leave." He wouldn't look at her. "I won't ever beg another woman to stay—not for me, my sons or my ranch." Now he did look at her, and Sara wished he hadn't. "I have my own dreams," he said.

Sara ran. She ran all the way to the house. Her truck was packed, filled with gas, ready since that morning and waiting for her in the drive. She yanked open the door and threw herself behind the wheel. She gripped the wheel and sat there, head pounding, out of breath, her chest heaving with barely controlled tears. The cool metal key dangled in the ignition, waiting for her.

Instead, she jerked the door handle and jumped to the ground. Running around to the camper, she scrambled inside and grabbed the plain cut-glass salt shaker from her tiny Formica table. She unscrewed the cheap metal lid and poured the salt onto the gravel. Nearly blind with tears, she ran up the porch stairs and into the kitchen. Fumbling with the key, she opened the glass front to the cabinet and sat her shaker on the shelf next to where the little black and white cow had been.

Swallowing hard, she stumbled to her truck. The engine started easily on the first try. She shoved it into gear with one hand, wiping tears with the other. Letting out the clutch, she guided the truck down the drive and turned north, toward Yellowstone.

Chapter Ten

Mac cut the engine and turned to the woman beside him. "Thanks for the evening, Libby. I had a good time."

"So did I."

The night air stole through the cab, silky and cool. He breathed deeply, taking in the scents of summer—settling dust, old straw, freshly watered lawn—overlaid by the rich, dusky scent of Libby's perfume. Carl's old yellow Lab raised his head from his paws long enough to bark once or twice from the porch but didn't put too much energy into it.

"We'll have to do this more often." Mac tried, but he feared he didn't sound much more enthusiastic than the dog.

"Sure. Anytime you need a safe date, just let me know. I always appreciate a restaurant meal."

"Safe?" A contrary streak of stubbornness made him pretend he didn't understand.

But Libby's small chuckle let him know she saw right through him. "One that's still in love with her ex-husband, so she doesn't mind if you talk about another woman all night."

"I didn't—" He stopped. Yes, he had. He'd talked about Sara every minute, just like he'd thought about Sara every minute, every second since she'd driven away yesterday morning.

And the fact that he couldn't stop thinking about her had made him mad. He'd taken it out on pretty much anyone and anything around him. He'd snapped at the boys when they'd finally crawled out of bed. They'd snapped back just as readily. So he'd put them to work changing the water on the west field when he knew they were still too sick to do it, then yelled at them some more when they couldn't finish. Nobody touched the tuna noodle casserole he fixed for supper—he'd thrown the whole sticky mess, pan and all, to the chickens.

Today hadn't been much better. Everywhere he turned, he stumbled over a reminder of Sara. Resolutely, he'd dumped the vases of wilting flowers down the sink, taking grim satisfaction in the way the garbage disposal tore at the delicate petals, sucking them down the black hole. He'd pulled out random towels from the ridiculously neat linen closet, purposely disrupting the ordered sets of four, matched by color and size. He'd set his coffee cup on the counter and defiantly left the stain, a brown ring that seemed to reproach him every time he entered the kitchen.

But no matter how much he ground, rearranged or stained, he still thought of Sara.

That afternoon, he'd found one of Grandma's salt shakers, a little Holstein he'd broken when he was about six or seven. Wondering how it had ended up at the station, he took it to the house and unlocked the oak cabinet Great-grandpa Wallace had made. In its place, he found a cheap glass shaker, the kind they sold at the variety store in town for two dollars a pair. He picked it up and ran his fingers over its smooth, sharp angles, so clean and sharp he wouldn't be surprised if they drew blood. Just like its owner had.

He'd placed the shaker on the shelf, hiding it behind the smiling cow content beside her matching bull pepper shaker. Then he'd turned his back on it, just as Sara had, and crossed to the phone next to the refrigerator to call Libby, to ask her out to supper. Sara was right. It was time to move on. Libby was a great woman, right there under his nose.

Except he'd spent the evening reminiscing about Sara. And his nose had wished for the delicate fragrance of old-fashioned roses instead of the heady scent of musk.

"Come on in," Libby said, opening the door and hopping from his truck. "We'll have another cup of coffee and I'll listen some more."

He followed her into her parents' house, chastised and determined to change the subject. He knew Libby still hurt from her divorce. She'd loved that man to distraction. The least he could do was return the favor by listening to her for awhile.

The light in the living room was on as they entered. Edith reclined in an easy chair, an old pink robe belted around her waist, her gray hair covered in some kind of net stocking that came to a little pointed knot on top. She held a mug of something hot and was blowing on its creamy surface.

"Good evening, children," she greeted them, taking a tentative sip. "Can I get you a cup of hot cocoa? Warm milk's supposed to help you sleep, you know."

"But the caffeine in the chocolate keeps you awake, Mother," Libby said, dropping onto the couch and gesturing for Mac to do the same. "I think they cancel each other out."

"That's all right." Edith smiled benevolently. "There's

something soothing about hot chocolate, even in the middle of the summer.'' She took another sip. ''So, Sara's gone, is she?'' she said in that same benign voice.

Mac flinched against the pain, unprepared. He was going to have to find some way to keep his heart from falling to his boots every time he heard her name. ''She left yesterday.''

''You going after her?''

He was even less prepared for that question. ''Of course not.'' But both women looked at him as if Edith had asked something sensible, something within the realm of sanity when he knew perfectly well such a thing would be insane.

''Why not?''

''Well...because, that's why not.'' He stumbled, trying to find the words to explain to these women that Sara had left him a salt shaker when he'd wanted her soul. ''Sara's— She's got problems she hasn't worked through yet. She's not ready to—''

''She's ready,'' Edith declared. She set her mug on the end table beside her and pulled the lever on the chair to propel herself upright. Cinching the belt tighter around her middle, like a warrior girding for battle, she told him, ''Sara wouldn't have been so easy to persuade to stay this long if she hadn't found something pretty darn interesting here.''

Mac shook his head. ''She was just trying to be helpful.''

''When the wanderlust is running high in a woman, there ain't nothing going to hold her back.'' Edith spoke with conviction. ''If she stuck around this long, there was a reason.''

''Then it wasn't me,'' he said, starting to feel defensive, ''because I asked her to stay.''

''Asked or told?'' Libby cut in. ''Did you give her some

breathing room, or did you start giving ultimatums like you did when we were kids?''

"Well—" He tried to remember their conversation at the station right after her daughter had left, but he could summon the feel of her in his arms, the honeyed taste of her, better than he could recall the words that had followed.

"Like I thought." Edith snorted. "She probably saw herself elbow deep in dishwater before she could blink an eye. No wonder she gave you the old sayonara." She leaned forward, as if physical proximity were necessary to convey the intensity of her words. "Didn't you give her any choices, Mac? A woman's got to have choices."

He knew how a fox felt, cornered by dogs, as Libby and her mother edged toward him, waiting for his answer. "I offered to go with her," he said lamely.

Edith shook her head, clearly exasperated. "Wouldn't work. When you're running, you have to run alone, or it's not running." She kicked back the footrest on the recliner and took up her mug again, washing her hands of him.

"Why did you ask her to stay, Mac?" Libby asked quietly, picking up the gauntlet her mother had dropped with unusual care, all bantering gone from her voice.

Why? He stared at the woman next to him on the sofa, but he didn't see the blonde in jeans and black turtleneck sweater who sat with a sports sandal tucked under her, watching him with sympathetic blue eyes. Why? He leaned his head against the sofa and gave in to the feelings he'd been trying so hard to deny.

"Because I love her," he said, as quiet as Libby.

"And did you tell Sara that? Did you tell her you love her?"

As he sat silently on the worn tweed sofa, shoulders slumped, hands tucked between his knees like an errant schoolboy, Edith and Libby exchanged glances.

"I'll stay with the boys tomorrow," Libby said, laying a comforting hand on his shoulder, "while you go after her."

Between the scene with Laura and the one with Mac, Sara was wrung out. She'd driven nonstop to Yellowstone yesterday and had spent today playing tourist. She'd wandered the footpath that meandered through boiling springs, their depths stained surreal colors of yellow, rust and olive, a palette of melting minerals. She'd dutifully waited for Old Faithful to do its thing and managed to snap two quick pictures before the geyser subsided. But the throngs of tourists, brought in by belching diesel buses, had intruded and she found herself wanting to push past them as they gawked, wanting to walk in front of their poised cameras instead of politely waiting while they focused.

She was restless—and she was lonely. The last realization had sent her scurrying for the safety of her truck. She aimlessly drove the backroads of the national park, leaving behind the tourists, trying to drive beyond the loneliness. Trying to outrun the unease that gnawed at her, the growing fear that it wasn't working this time. Because when she'd driven away from the ranch yesterday, there was none of the sublime sense of freedom she'd felt the day she'd driven away from her Denver home, none of the joy she always felt on starting a new leg of her journey. Instead, she felt worse with every mile she went—every mile she put between herself and Mac.

She needed time to acclimate herself again to life on the road, she told herself firmly, gripping the steering wheel more comfortably, trying to mold it to her hands until it felt familiar again. She pulled at the strap that rested across her shoulder, nudging it aside so it didn't rub so painfully against her neck. She willed herself to focus on the majestic beauty around her, to appreciate the quiet, the only sound the whip of the wind as it came through the open window of the truck, the hum of the tires eating up the miles.

She shifted restlessly. The hum sounded more like a drone, dully repetitive, and the wind assaulted her, flicking annoying strands of hair across her face. She raised a knee to hold the wheel steady while she used both hands to smooth her hair into the band that held it away from her face. She glanced in the rearview mirror, hardly noticing the reflected sunset behind her, seeing only the scattered gray beginning to sneak through the brown at her temples.

She jerked her eyes away, concentrating on the road. It stretched before her, pine trees towering on either side, a green tunnel in the darkening gloom of early evening. The broken yellow line flashed by like a strobe light flickering at the edge of her sight, pulling her forward, on and on into the tunnel. Suddenly she longed for a rise in the road, a high point where she could see over the trees, see to the horizon, uninterrupted—like she could on the ranch.

Her foot pressed the brake without conscious direction. The truck slowed and she guided it toward the edge of the pavement. *I don't want to go down this new road anymore.* The thought stunned her. She sat very still and tested it again. *I have no desire to go ahead, no curiosity as to what might be around the next bend.* She waited in the gathering twilight, trying to assimilate the feelings that threatened to overwhelm her. Her mind was blank, no coherent thoughts came together, no great revelation broke through, no moment of great insight, yet as she carefully eased the truck into gear and made a wide turn in the road, heading toward the campgrounds, she understood she'd just made a momentous decision. One she wasn't ready to examine too closely just yet.

It was dark by the time she pulled into her assigned camping spot. She climbed from the truck, stiff from sitting so long, and looked around her as she stretched. Army surplus tents, pup tents, battered campers, elaborate recreational vehicles, dozens of other campers surrounded her, the lights of their fires outlining their campsites only a few dozen feet apart. In the middle of Wyoming she would sleep closer to other people than she would in a hotel in downtown Denver.

She climbed the stairs into her camper, pulled the door shut behind her and flicked on the little light above the sink. This was her home, she told herself as she stood with the sink on one side of her, the table on the other, the bed directly in front and the door behind. She took a deep breath and closed her eyes, willing herself to feel the coziness, the familiarity, the contentment. But when she opened them, the camper seemed just as hot and cramped and claustrophobic as it had last night when she'd tossed and turned for hours in the confines of the metal shell.

Dispirited, she slid onto the padded seat hooked to the table and leaned her elbows on its top. Maybe she'd just go to bed. She wasn't really hungry. Dishes from last night and this morning sat in the sink, the milk from her cereal a flaking white ring in the bottom of the bowl. A flap of pastel sheet peeked from the bottom of the floral bedspread she'd pulled haphazardly in place. She been too tired and depressed to do any more last night, or this morning, either. And she hadn't given it a thought during the day.

She squinted at the mess around her, trying to remember. But there'd been no niggling in the back of her mind, no sense of wrongness, of something left undone, no urge to put things in shipshape order before starting the day. She'd gotten through her day just fine, thank you, with milk souring in her sink. She rested her head on her hands. As far as she was concerned, those dishes could stay there forever. She was simply too tired, too heartsick, to care anymore.

Suddenly, she gave a muffled laugh. She didn't care! Not a bit. She raised her head and looked around her. It was as if blinders had been lifted, and for the first time in years she saw the difference between what was important and what was not. And, by God, those dishes weren't important—not compared to her love for Mac. And that sloppy bed wasn't important—not compared to Mac. Another strangled little laugh bubbled up. It had taken nothing less than a broken heart to beat her compulsion.

She didn't care about dishes, she cared about Mac.

Edith's words from yesterday morning repeated themselves in her head. *It's okay to care, as long as you get to choose what you care about.* She slid from behind the table and pushed open the camper door, letting in the cool night air. Dropping to the floor in the open doorway, she hung her legs outside, kicking her heels against the bumper while she pondered the things she'd chosen to care about in her life.

She'd freely chosen to marry Greg, and she'd loved him the way a nineteen-year-old loves, without any idea of what marriage really meant. It had all been overwhelming to a girl who'd only wanted to be a cowgirl. The demands of their insulated university life had been so gradual, so insidious— She'd been told to care about those stupid faculty teas, she realized suddenly. It hadn't been by choice. Greg had told her how important crustless cucumber sandwiches were, and she hadn't known enough to question him.

But now? Now she clearly understood the enormous amount of work required to keep a household running—and to help raise two teenage boys. Now she knew all about what would be expected of her. What if she were to consciously and freely *choose* to do it? Would it be different if she had a choice as to what to care about?

Her thoughts spun faster and faster as her whole life

rewrote itself in her mind, her past colored by this new light. What if she were to go back and ask Mac to come with her to Yellowstone? What if her offer led to matching china and bake sales and mowing that enormous ranch lawn? She felt no twinge of horror at the thought—only anticipation. The freedom of the open road was a wonderful thing, she saw, but no commitment and no responsibilities also meant no love.

She had to go back. Thank God the road went both ways, she thought, getting to her feet with renewed vigor. Tomorrow morning, she'd start for home.

Tonight, she was going to find herself a real bed to sleep in, in a room with a high ceiling and a hot shower. She jumped into the truck and drove to the historic old lodge in the center of the park. It was almost ten o'clock. Maybe they'd have a last-minute cancellation or a no-show.

The doors to the lodge stood open, a bright square of light in the massive log building. Sara entered, her eyes drawn instantly to the ceiling so far overhead. The center lobby was open from floor to roof, the rooms located around the perimeter with open walkways overlooking the public area. Huge stained logs formed support columns, so tall it was difficult to believe they'd once been living trees. There were still a number of tourists milling about, cameras a permanent fixture around their necks, browsing through the gift shop or gawking at the architecture as she did.

Pulling her eyes to ground level, she started for the reservation desk. From the corner of her eye, she saw a woman leaving the gift shop, head down, leafing through some postcards in her hand. The familiar curly hair made Sara stop in her tracks.

"Laura?"

At the sound of her name, Laura lifted her head. A smile

lit her face. She tucked the postcards into her purse and hurried across the lobby.

"Surprised you again, huh? I'm like that bad penny that keeps popping up."

"Laura, what are you *doing* here?" Sara asked, flabbergasted.

The young woman shrugged and a slight flush stained her cheeks. "I thought I'd give your open-road thing a try. You know, just take off and spend a few days seeing the sights. I camped out last night."

"But you *hate* to camp."

"Yeah, it was pretty awful, all right. But I wanted to give you the benefit of the doubt." She began to chew on her bottom lip. "I—I never thought I'd run into you here with all the tourists. I thought I'd wait until I got this all straight in my mind, then the next time you called I could tell you..."

"Tell me what?" Sara felt as confused as her daughter sounded. "Come over here, let's sit down." She led them to two chairs partially shielded by a towering column.

"Now, what's this all about?" She couldn't remember the last time she'd seen Laura this serious. And where was the antagonism?

"I just want to apologize, Mom," Laura began, twisting her fingers in her lap.

"Oh, no, sweetheart. It's been a tough time for you. I understand—"

"It's been a tough time for you, too," Laura interrupted. "But these last two years, I've spent a lot of time feeling sorry for myself, feeling like I'd lost both my father and my mother."

"Oh, baby—" Sara couldn't stand it, couldn't stand to think of the pain she'd caused her daughter. She started to reach out, but Laura drew back.

"That's the point, Mom. I'm not a baby anymore, and

it's time I grew up. After I left you yesterday, I drove around and around, trying to think this all out. I just can't keep on the way I have been, fighting all the time. It hurts too much.''

"I know."

"I've always thought this was all your fault, that you were the one doing this to us, but I realized that I was asking you to make all the sacrifices for me without me doing anything in return. So I decided to head up here to give this traveling thing a try. I thought if you couldn't come to me, maybe I could come to you—join you in your travels or something." Tears were very close to the surface. "I tried, Mom. I really tried. I was a free spirit for two days and I hated it."

Sara laughed gently and gathered her daughter close. This time Laura allowed herself to be drawn into the warm circle. "The important thing is that you tried. And you did it for me. That means so much to me. And you want to know something?"

Laura sniffed. "What?"

"I think it's losing its appeal for me, too."

"What!" Sara saw hope flare in her daughter's eyes, wet with unshed tears.

"That's why I came to the lodge. I wanted to get a room. I couldn't stand the thought of sleeping in the camper tonight."

"Sorry, but I got their last available room." Laura's smile was her mischievous grin of old, and she wiped at her nose with the back of her hand as she sat up straight. "I wouldn't mind a roommate, though."

"That would be wonderful, sweetheart. Thank you." She hugged her daughter and for the first time in a long time, Laura didn't stiffen, but returned the hug.

They got up and started to walk toward the elevator. "I've only got the room for tonight," Laura said. "I'm going back to Denver tomorrow.'' She paused, and Sara knew it was her way of asking her plans.

"I'm leaving tomorrow, too.'' She pushed the elevator button, hesitating to broach the subject that might alienate her daughter all over again. "Laura, I know you didn't have much time to get to know him, but—"

"Ah.'' Laura nodded knowingly. "Mac. You're going back to him.''

It was a statement, not a question, but Sara found herself nodding. "I don't know where it will lead, but—"

"I do. I could see the sparks fly between you two the second he hopped into the room yesterday. In fact, I could tell from your phone calls something serious was going on. That's the main reason I came barreling up to Dutch Creek like some jealous teenager with all that you're-not-my-father baloney going round in my head.''

She held up her hand, stopping Sara from responding. "Don't worry. It didn't last long. Even I'm not *that* childish.'' She looked at her mother curiously. "You going to marry him?''

"If he asks.'' The elevator doors opened and they stepped inside. They were silent and Sara began to tense. "Laura—"

"Daddy's been dead a long time now. I want you to be happy. And if Mac Wallace makes you happy, it's fine by me.'' She looked sharply at her mother. "Does he like to travel?''

"I don't think so. He's too busy.''

"I like the man already,'' Laura said with certainty.

Mac's powerful truck ate up the miles as he headed north. His crutches lay flung across the seat beside him. He grumbled whenever he had to press the clutch with his casted foot, but he was managing so far. Once he got there, it might be another matter. Yellowstone had a lot of campgrounds. He'd just have to keep looking until he found her truck, he told himself, glad Libby had offered to watch the boys. He planned to search until he found her and stay with her until he'd convinced her to come back with him.

Without frightening her this time, he reminded himself sternly. Just put a limit on it, he thought, rehearsing what he would say in his mind, oblivious to the countryside speeding past. He'd try to wean her from the road gradually. Ask her to stay just a few weeks or however long she could manage. Or ask her to plan her travels so she stopped by now and then, until she got comfortable. Or maybe—

Hell. He pounded the wheel with the heel of his hand. He'd take whatever crumbs she had to offer. He wanted her, heart, body and soul, but he loved her so much he would take whatever she could give—a month, a week, a day, an hour. He'd take it and thank God for it.

Once again, he cursed the stupid pride that had forced Sara away. His pride had been so wounded by Ronda's rejection that he'd demanded one-hundred-percent total commitment from a woman. He'd wanted it in writing that Sara wouldn't leave him, that she'd love every blade of grass and nail in the place. What choice had she had but to run, faced with that kind of all-or-nothing attitude?

She'd said she was afraid of the future. But he hadn't listened, hadn't reassured her, hadn't searched for a compromise. His pride had demanded everything, and now he had nothing. But he no longer had any pride when it came to Sara. If he could just find her and convince her to give him a chance.

He'd left Dutch Creek in the dust and kept driving, concentrating on the strip of asphalt rushing under his tires in a gray blur. His body reacted to the passing truck and camper before his mind registered the make and color. His foot automatically hit the brake, moving so fast his boot knocked against his cast. His eyes flew to the big side mirror mounted on his door. In it, he saw the brake light flash red on the truck behind him, as it, too, slowed and pulled over to the shoulder.

He ground the gears into reverse and backed up until he was even with the other truck. He jumped out, leaving the door hanging open behind him. Eschewing crutches, he ran, hobbling as best he could toward Sara, who had jumped down and was running to meet him on the side of the road.

Sara stopped a few feet from him, suddenly uncertain. She watched Mac stop, too, arms that had been outstretched toward her dropping to his side.

"Sara," he greeted, his head making a little bob.

"Mac," she returned just as formally, all the time thinking how wonderful he looked with his hat tipped low, his blue striped shirt rolled from his wrists, his jeans faded and tight. All the time wondering what he was doing on the road this far north. She'd stopped instinctively when she'd recognized his truck, her heart jumping to conclusions her mind now asked her to verify.

"Yellowstone's that way." He jerked his head behind him, back toward his truck.

"I know. I've been there."

"Nothing much the way you're headed now but a ranch or two."

"I know. I've been there, too." She swallowed, needing to know. "You're a long way from home."

"I was going to find someone. How about you? What brings you this way?"

Her heart gave a slam in her chest. "Same reason. I was looking for someone."

He nodded and stared over her head, studying something in the distance with apparent fascination. "When I found my someone—the person I was looking for—I was going to tell her that I loved her."

Tears sprang to her eyes, and she put a hand over her mouth to suppress a cry.

"I was going to ask her to marry me." His eyes found hers. "I was going to remind her that a highway goes right in front of my place. I was going to tell her I'd keep her truck tuned up and filled with gas so she could take off whenever she needed to—as long as she came back to me whenever she could."

Tears rolled unchecked down her cheeks. "I—I was going to tell my someone that I loved him, too, and that the road was so lonely without him. I was going to tell him—"

She never got to finish her sentence. Mac swept her into his arms, his hat falling to the ground, his mouth covering hers, welcoming her back where she belonged. The strength of his arms lifted her off her feet, and she felt their bodies sway as he balanced them on his good foot. But she didn't take her lips from his. She didn't care if they landed in a sprawl on the side of the road—as long as he never let her go.

"What are you doing?" she asked many minutes later as he left her mouth to bury his face in her hair, breathing deeply.

"Smelling you."

She laughed and sniffled and he kissed her tears and wiped them away with his thumbs, cupping her face while she smiled at him.

"I'll do whatever it takes to make you happy, Sara," he said, and she could see the vow reflected in his eyes. "I'll hire a housekeeper so you won't feel so pressured, I'll learn to make a casserole with something besides tuna, I'll pack your bags when you need to go—"

She stood on tiptoe and pressed her mouth to his to stop his fervent promises. "I'm not going anywhere," she told him. She linked their fingers together. "The only place I'll be running to from now on—is running home to you."

Epilogue

"The reason they call it fall break is for you to take a break. It's too early to study, anyway."

Sara heard Mac move behind her where she sat on a log close to the campfire, warding off the early morning chill. His hand came to rest on her shoulder, solid and possessive, and the aroma of coffee moved tantalizingly close. She looked up and smiled, raising her face for his kiss, tasting bacon and wood smoke and mint toothpaste.

"I don't want to get behind, that's all." She closed the heavy biology textbook balanced on her knees and took the mug of coffee he offered her. Luxuriating in its warmth, she snuggled it between her palms.

"You aced the first test," he reminded her. "Your professor thinks you're a genius."

"Hmph. My professor looks about Michael's age on the tapes and has no idea I'm old enough to be his grandmother." She took a sip of coffee. "Or that I'll probably be the oldest graduate from veterinary college in the history of the university."

She'd enrolled that fall at the university in Cheyenne, receiving weekly packets of class videotapes, talking to the professor by phone and returning her assignments by mail. Years of study stretched before her, but it was the most exhilarating challenge she'd faced in a long, long time. And Mac had encouraged her every step of the way.

"You'll be mature and wise when you graduate, and all the ranchers will take their animals to you instead of some wet-behind-the-ears kid." He dropped another kiss on her lips, then straightened. "Now it's time to hit the road."

"Speaking of taking a break, you still haven't gotten the hang of this vacation thing, have you?" she teased. "We don't have to start before sunrise every morning."

"Hey, this is the first vacation I've had in fifteen years. I'm new at this."

She smiled as she watched him empty the coffeepot onto the last of the embers still glowing from their breakfast fire. He'd put on a couple of pounds since the wedding, she thought, liking the way her cooking looked on him. Stretching out her legs and crossing her hiking boots at the ankle, she watched him break camp, enjoying the sight. It was nice, very nice, to have someone else do the things she'd had to do so often for herself. She'd been convinced a solitary trip was the only journey worth taking, but these precious days with Mac had shown her how wrong she'd been.

The heavy mist of the Oregon coast swirled low among the pines, enclosing their campsite in a protective cocoon that muffled the sound of the ocean at the base of the nearby cliffs. The wet, heavy air smelled of sap and salt and humus, a subtle but constant reminder that the open spaces of Wyoming were far, far away.

"Do you think we should stop someplace and give Laura a call?" she asked, surprised by the unfamiliar stab of homesickness. She got to her feet and brushed bits of bark from her jeans.

"It might be a good idea." Mac climbed the stairs into the camper and began to store the breakfast dishes. "She seemed a little shook up after that deal with the washing machine. It was great of her to offer to stay with the boys while we're gone, but I hope it's not going to be too much for her."

Joining him inside the camper, she squeezed past and reached for the rumpled sheets on the bed. "It will do her good. A little cooking, a little cleaning, a few kids—she's always thought it was so easy. She might look at her dear mother with new respect by the time we get back." Her hands stilled as she fluffed a pillow. "Is today Tuesday or Wednesday?"

"Tuesday—I think."

"Oh, good. Still a week before Cyrus and Susie's wedding."

"Plenty of time," Mac agreed. He turned in the cramped space to wrap his arms around her waist and pull her back against him. "So why don't you forget about making that bed? You know we're going to spend most of the week in it, anyway." He began to nuzzle the side of her neck.

She twisted in his arms to face him. "You might have a point, cowboy. I'd hate to go to all that trouble if you've got other plans."

"Damn right I do." His lips had worked their way up to her temple. "Which way do you want to go today?" he murmured against her skin. "North or south?"

"Uh..." It was hard to concentrate when he did that with his hands. "Uh..."

"I take that to mean you're open to suggestions?"

She tried to nod.

"Then—" his lips nibbled "—I think we should—" they tugged "—stay right here."

And as they sank onto the bed, creasing the floral print bedspread and mussing the pillows, Sara couldn't have agreed more.

* * * * *

Available in February 1998

ANN MAJOR

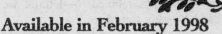

CHILDREN OF DESTINY
When Passion and Fate Intertwine...

SECRET CHILD

Although everyone told Jack West that his wife,
Chantal —the woman who'd betrayed him and sent
him to prison for a crime he didn't commit —had
died, Jack knew she'd merely transformed herself
into supermodel Mischief Jones. But when he
finally captured the woman he'd been hunting,
she denied everything. Who was she really —
an angel or a cunningly brilliant counterfeit?"

"Want it all? Read Ann Major."
—Nora Roberts, *New York Times*
bestselling author

Don't miss this compelling story,
available at your favorite retail outlet.
Only from Silhouette books.

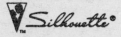

Take 4 bestselling love stories FREE

Plus get a FREE surprise gift!

Special Limited-time Offer

Mail to Silhouette Reader Service™

3010 Walden Avenue
P.O. Box 1867
Buffalo, N.Y. 14240-1867

YES! Please send me 4 free Silhouette Romance™ novels and my free surprise gift. Then send me 6 brand-new novels every month, which I will receive months before they appear in bookstores. Bill me at the low price of $2.67 each plus 25¢ delivery and applicable sales tax, if any.* That's the complete price and a savings of over 10% off the cover prices—quite a bargain! I understand that accepting the books and gift places me under no obligation ever to buy any books. I can always return a shipment and cancel at any time. Even if I never buy another book from Silhouette, the 4 free books and the surprise gift are mine to keep forever.

215 BPA A3UT

Name	(PLEASE PRINT)	
Address		Apt. No.
City	State	Zip

Return to the Towers!

In March
New York Times bestselling author

NORA ROBERTS

brings us to the Calhouns' fabulous
Maine coast mansion and reveals the
tragic secrets hidden there for generations.

For all his degrees, Professor Max Quartermain has a
lot to learn about love—and luscious Lilah Calhoun is
just the woman to teach him. Ex-cop Holt Bradford is
as prickly as a thornbush—until Suzanna Calhoun's
special touch makes love blossom in his heart.
And all of them are caught in the race to solve
the generations-old mystery of a priceless
lost necklace...and a timeless love.

Lilah and Suzanna
THE
Calhoun Women

**A special 2-in-1 edition containing
FOR THE LOVE OF LILAH and
SUZANNA'S SURRENDER**

Available at your favorite retail outlet.

Look us up on-line at: http://www.romance.net   CWVOL2

He's more than a man, he's one of our

Fabulous Fathers

Join Silhouette Romance as we present these heartwarming tales about wonderful men facing the challenges of fatherhood and love.

January 1998:
THE BILLIONAIRE'S BABY CHASE by Valerie Parv (SR#1270)
Billionaire daddy James Langford finds himself falling for Zoe Holden, the alluring foster mother of his long-lost daughter.

March 1998:
IN CARE OF THE SHERIFF by Susan Meier (SR#1283)
Sexy sheriff Ryan Kelly becomes a father-in-training when he is stranded with beautiful Madison Delaney and her adorable baby.

May 1998:
FALLING FOR A FATHER OF FOUR by Arlene James (SR#1295)
Overwhelmed single father Orren Ellis is soon humming the wedding march after hiring new nanny Mattie Kincaid.

Fall in love with our FABULOUS FATHERS!
And be sure to look for additional FABULOUS FATHERS titles
in the months to come.

Available at your favorite retail outlet.

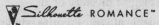